Sula

*Also by Toni Morrison
in Large Print:*

Beloved
Paradise
The Bluest Eye

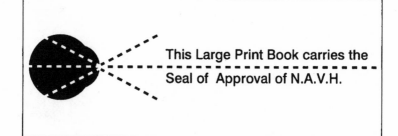

SULA

Toni Morrison

Thorndike Press • Waterville, Maine

Published in 2002 by arrangement with Alfred A. Knopf, Inc.

Thorndike Press Large Print Basic Series.

The tree indicium is a trademark of Thorndike Press.

The text of this Large Print edition is unabridged.
Other aspects of the book may vary from the original edition.

Set in 16 pt. Plantin by Elena Picard.

Printed in the United States on permanent paper.

Library of Congress Cataloging-in-Publication Data

Morrison, Toni.
    Sula / Toni Morrison.
       p. cm.
    ISBN 0-7862-4653-7 (lg. print : hc : alk. paper)
    1. African American women — Fiction. 2. City and
town life — Fiction. 3. Female friendship — Fiction.
4. Ohio — Fiction. 5. Large type books. I. Title.
PS3563.O8749 S8 2002
813'.54—dc21   2002027198

It is sheer good fortune to miss somebody long before they leave you. This book is for Ford and Slade, whom I miss although they have not left me.

"Nobody knew my rose of the world but me. . . . I had too much glory. They don't want glory like that *in nobody's heart."*

— The Rose Tattoo

PART ONE

In that place, where they tore the nightshade and blackberry patches from their roots to make room for the Medallion City Golf Course, there was once a neighborhood. It stood in the hills above the valley town of Medallion and spread all the way to the river. It is called the suburbs now, but when black people lived there it was called the Bottom. One road, shaded by beeches, oaks, maples and chestnuts, connected it to the valley. The beeches are gone now, and so are the pear trees where children sat and yelled down through the blossoms to passersby. Generous funds have been allotted to level the stripped and faded buildings that clutter the road from Medallion up to the golf course. They are going to raze the Time and a Half Pool Hall, where feet in long tan shoes once pointed down from chair rungs. A steel ball will knock to dust Irene's Palace of Cosmetology, where women used to lean their heads back on sink trays and doze while Irene lathered Nu Nile into their hair. Men in khaki work clothes will pry loose the slats of Reba's Grill, where the owner cooked in her hat because she couldn't remember the ingredients without it.

There will be nothing left of the Bottom (the footbridge that crossed the river is already gone), but perhaps it is just as well, since it wasn't a town anyway: just a neighborhood where on quiet days people in valley houses could hear singing sometimes, banjos sometimes, and, if a valley man happened to have business up in those hills — collecting rent or insurance payments — he might see a dark woman in a flowered dress doing a bit of cakewalk, a bit of black bottom, a bit of "messing around" to the lively notes of a mouth organ. Her bare feet would raise the saffron dust that floated down on the coveralls and bunion-split shoes of the man breathing music in and out of his harmonica. The black people watching her would laugh and rub their knees, and it would be easy for the valley man to hear the laughter and not notice the adult pain that rested somewhere under the eyelids, somewhere under their head rags and soft felt hats, somewhere in the palm of the

10

hand, somewhere behind the frayed lapels, somewhere in the sinew's curve. He'd have to stand in the back of Greater Saint Matthew's and let the tenor's voice dress him in silk, or touch the hands of the spoon carvers (who had not worked in eight years) and let the fingers that danced on wood kiss his skin. Otherwise the pain would escape him even though the laughter was part of the pain.

A shucking, knee-slapping, wet-eyed laughter that could even describe and explain how they came to be where they were.

A joke. A nigger joke. That was the way it got started. Not the town, of course, but that part of town where the Negroes lived, the part they called the Bottom in spite of the fact that it was up in the hills. Just a nigger joke. The kind white folks tell when the mill closes down and they're looking for a little comfort somewhere. The kind colored folks tell on themselves when the rain doesn't come, or comes for weeks, and they're looking for a little comfort somehow.

A good white farmer promised freedom and a piece of bottom land to his slave if he would perform some very difficult chores. When the slave completed the work, he asked the farmer to keep his end of the bargain. Freedom was easy — the farmer had no objection to that. But he didn't want to give up any land. So he told the slave that he was very sorry that he had to give him valley land. He had hoped to give him a piece of the Bottom. The slave blinked and said he thought valley land was bottom land. The master said, "Oh, no! See those hills? That's bottom land, rich and fertile."

"But it's high up in the hills," said the slave.

"High up from us," said the master, "but when God looks down, it's the bottom. That's why we call it so. It's the bottom of heaven — best land there is."

So the slave pressed his master to try to get him some. He preferred it to the valley. And it was done. The nigger got the hilly land, where planting was backbreaking, where the soil slid down and washed away the seeds, and where the wind lingered all through the winter.

Which accounted for the fact that white people lived on the rich valley floor in that little river town in Ohio, and the blacks populated the hills above it, taking small consolation in the fact that every day they could literally look down on the white folks.

Still, it was lovely up in the Bottom. After the town grew and the farm land turned into a village and the village into a town and the streets of Medallion were hot and dusty with progress, those heavy trees that sheltered the shacks up in the Bottom were wonderful to see. And the hunters who went there sometimes wondered in private if maybe the white farmer was right after all. Maybe it was the bottom of heaven.

The black people would have disagreed, but they had no time to think about it. They were mightily preoccupied with earthly things — and each other, wondering even as early as 1920 what Shadrack was all about, what that little girl Sula who grew into a woman in their town was all about, and what they themselves were all about, tucked up there in the Bottom.

1919

Except for World War II, nothing ever interfered with the celebration of National Suicide Day. It had taken place every January third since 1920, although Shadrack, its founder, was for many years the only celebrant. Blasted and permanently astonished by the events of 1917, he had returned to Medallion handsome but ravaged, and even the most fastidious people in the town sometimes caught themselves dreaming of what he must have been like a few years back before he went off to war. A young man of hardly twenty, his head full of nothing and his mouth recalling the taste of lipstick, Shadrack had found himself in December, 1917, running with his comrades across a field in France. It was his first encounter with the enemy and he didn't know whether his company was running toward them or away. For several days they had been marching, keeping close to a stream that was

14

frozen at its edges. At one point they crossed it, and no sooner had he stepped foot on the other side than the day was adangle with shouts and explosions. Shellfire was all around him, and though he knew that this was something called *it*, he could not muster up the proper feeling — the feeling that would accommodate *it*. He expected to be terrified or exhilarated — to feel *something* very strong. In fact, he felt only the bite of a nail in his boot, which pierced the ball of his foot whenever he came down on it. The day was cold enough to make his breath visible, and he wondered for a moment at the purity and whiteness of his own breath among the dirty, gray explosions surrounding him. He ran, bayonet fixed, deep in the great sweep of men flying across this field. Wincing at the pain in his foot, he turned his head a little to the right and saw the face of a soldier near him fly off. Before he could register shock, the rest of the soldier's head disappeared under the inverted soup bowl of his helmet. But stubbornly, taking no direction from the brain, the body of the headless soldier ran on, with energy and grace, ignoring altogether the drip and slide of brain tissue down its back.

When Shadrack opened his eyes he was

propped up in a small bed. Before him on a tray was a large tin plate divided into three triangles. In one triangle was rice, in another meat, and in the third stewed tomatoes. A small round depression held a cup of whitish liquid. Shadrack stared at the soft colors that filled these triangles: the lumpy whiteness of rice, the quivering blood tomatoes, the grayish-brown meat. All their repugnance was contained in the neat balance of the triangles — a balance that soothed him, transferred some of its equilibrium to him. Thus reassured that the white, the red and the brown would stay where they were — would not explode or burst forth from their restricted zones — he suddenly felt hungry and looked around for his hands. His glance was cautious at first, for he had to be very careful — anything could be anywhere. Then he noticed two lumps beneath the beige blanket on either side of his hips. With extreme care he lifted one arm and was relieved to find his hand attached to his wrist. He tried the other and found it also. Slowly he directed one hand toward the cup and, just as he was about to spread his fingers, they began to grow in higgledy-piggledy fashion like Jack's beanstalk all over the tray and the bed. With a shriek he

16

closed his eyes and thrust his huge growing hands under the covers. Once out of sight they seemed to shrink back to their normal size. But the yell had brought a male nurse.

"Private? We're not going to have any trouble today, are we? Are we, Private?"

Shadrack looked up at a balding man dressed in a green-cotton jacket and trousers. His hair was parted low on the right side so that some twenty or thirty yellow hairs could discreetly cover the nakedness of his head.

"Come on. Pick up that spoon. Pick it up, Private. Nobody is going to feed you forever."

Sweat slid from Shadrack's armpits down his sides. He could not bear to see his hands grow again and he was frightened of the voice in the apple-green suit.

"Pick it up, I said. There's no point to this . . ." The nurse reached under the cover for Shadrack's wrist to pull out the monstrous hand. Shadrack jerked it back and overturned the tray. In panic he raised himself to his knees and tried to fling off and away his terrible fingers, but succeeded only in knocking the nurse into the next bed.

When they bound Shadrack into a strait-

17

jacket, he was both relieved and grateful, for his hands were at last hidden and confined to whatever size they had attained.

Laced and silent in his small bed, he tried to tie the loose cords in his mind. He wanted desperately to see his own face and connect it with the word "private" — the word the nurse (and the others who helped bind him) had called him. "Private" he thought was something secret, and he wondered why they looked at him and called him a secret. Still, if his hands behaved as they had done, what might he expect from his face? The fear and longing were too much for him, so he began to think of other things. That is, he let his mind slip into whatever cave mouths of memory it chose.

He saw a window that looked out on a river which he knew was full of fish. Someone was speaking softly just outside the door . . .

Shadrack's earlier violence had coincided with a memorandum from the hospital executive staff in reference to the distribution of patients in high-risk areas. There was clearly a demand for space. The priority or the violence earned Shadrack his release, $217 in cash, a full suit of

18

clothes and copies of very official-looking papers.

When he stepped out of the hospital door the grounds overwhelmed him: the cropped shrubbery, the edged lawns, the undeviating walks. Shadrack looked at the cement stretches: each one leading clear-headedly to some presumably desirable destination. There were no fences, no warnings, no obstacles at all between concrete and green grass, so one could easily ignore the tidy sweep of stone and cut out in another direction — a direction of one's own.

Shadrack stood at the foot of the hospital steps watching the heads of trees tossing ruefully but harmlessly, since their trunks were rooted too deeply in the earth to threaten him. Only the walks made him uneasy. He shifted his weight, wondering how he could get to the gate without stepping on the concrete. While plotting his course — where he would have to leap, where to skirt a clump of bushes — a loud guffaw startled him. Two men were going up the steps. Then he noticed that there were many people about, and that he was just now seeing them, or else they had just materialized. They were thin slips, like paper dolls floating down the walks. Some

19

were seated in chairs with wheels, propelled by other paper figures from behind. All seemed to be smoking, and their arms and legs curved in the breeze. A good high wind would pull them up and away and they would land perhaps among the tops of the trees.

Shadrack took the plunge. Four steps and he was on the grass heading for the gate. He kept his head down to avoid seeing the paper people swerving and bending here and there, and he lost his way. When he looked up, he was standing by a low red building separated from the main building by a covered walkway. From somewhere came a sweetish smell which reminded him of something painful. He looked around for the gate and saw that he had gone directly away from it in his complicated journey over the grass. Just to the left of the low building was a graveled driveway that appeared to lead outside the grounds. He trotted quickly to it and left, at last, a haven of more than a year, only eight days of which he fully recollected.

Once on the road, he headed west. The long stay in the hospital had left him weak — too weak to walk steadily on the gravel shoulders of the road. He shuffled, grew dizzy, stopped for breath, started again, stumbling and sweating but refusing to wipe his temples, still afraid to look at his hands. Passengers in dark, square cars shuttered their eyes at what they took to be a drunken man.

The sun was already directly over his head when he came to a town. A few blocks of shaded streets and he was already at its heart — a pretty, quietly regulated downtown.

Exhausted, his feet clotted with pain, he sat down at the curbside to take off his shoes. He closed his eyes to avoid seeing his hands and fumbled with the laces of the heavy high-topped shoes. The nurse had tied them into a double knot, the way one does for children, and Shadrack, long unaccustomed to the manipulation of intricate things, could not get them loose. Uncoordinated, his fingernails tore away at the knots. He fought a rising hysteria that was not merely anxiety to free his aching feet; his very life depended on the release of the knots. Suddenly without raising his eyelids, he began to cry. Twenty-two years old, weak, hot, frightened, not daring to acknowledge the fact that he didn't even know who or what he was . . . with no past, no language, no tribe, no source, no address book, no comb, no pencil, no clock, no pocket handkerchief, no rug, no bed, no can opener, no faded postcard, no soap, no key, no tobacco pouch, no soiled underwear and nothing nothing nothing to do . . . he was sure of one thing only: the unchecked monstrosity of his hands. He cried soundlessly at the curbside of a small Midwestern town wondering where the window was, and the river, and the soft voices just outside the door . . .

Through his tears he saw the fingers joining the laces, tentatively at first, then rapidly. The four fingers of each hand fused into the fabric, knotted themselves and zigzagged in and out of the tiny eyeholes.

By the time the police drove up, Shadrack was suffering from a blinding headache, which was not abated by the comfort he felt when the policemen pulled his hands away from what he thought was a permanent entanglement with his shoelaces. They took him to jail, booked him for vagrancy and intoxication, and locked him in a cell. Lying on a cot, Shadrack could only stare helplessly at the wall, so paralyzing was the pain in his head. He lay in this agony for a long while and then realized he was staring at the painted-over letters of a command to fuck himself. He studied the phrase as the pain in his head subsided.

Like moonlight stealing under a window shade an idea insinuated itself: his earlier desire to see his own face. He looked for a mirror; there was none. Finally, keeping his hands carefully behind his back he made his way to the toilet bowl and peeped in. The water was unevenly lit by the sun so he could make nothing out. Returning to his cot he took the blanket and covered his head, rendering the water dark enough to see his reflection. There in the toilet water he saw a grave black face. A black so definite, so unequivocal, it astonished him. He had been harboring a skittish apprehension that he was not real — that he didn't exist at all. But when the blackness greeted him with its indisputable presence, he wanted nothing more. In his joy he took the risk of letting one edge of the blanket drop and glanced at his hands. They were still. Courteously still.

Shadrack rose and returned to the cot, where he fell into the first sleep of his new life. A sleep deeper than the hospital drugs; deeper than the pits of plums, steadier than the condor's wing; more tranquil than the curve of eggs.

The sheriff looked through the bars at the young man with the matted hair. He had read through his prisoner's papers and hailed a farmer. When Shadrack awoke, the sheriff handed him back his papers and escorted him to the back of a wagon. Shadrack got in and in less than three hours he was back in Medallion, for he had been only twenty-two miles from his window, his river, and his soft voices just outside the door.

In the back of the wagon, supported by sacks of squash and hills of pumpkins, Shadrack began a struggle that was to last for twelve days, a struggle to order and focus experience. It had to do with making a place for fear as a way of controlling it. He knew the smell of death and was terrified of it, for he could not anticipate it. It was not death or dying that frightened him, but the unexpectedness of both. In sorting it all out, he hit on the notion that if one day a year were devoted to it, everybody could get it out of the way and the rest of the year would be safe and free. In this manner he instituted National Suicide Day.

On the third day of the new year, he walked through the Bottom down Carpenter's Road with a cowbell and a hangman's rope calling the people together. Telling them that this was their only chance to kill themselves or each other.

At first the people in the town were frightened; they knew Shadrack was crazy but that did not mean that he didn't have any sense or, even more important, that he had no power. His eyes were so wild, his hair so long and matted, his voice was so full of authority and thunder that he caused panic on the first, or Charter, National Suicide Day in 1920. The next one, in 1921, was less frightening but still worrisome. The people had seen him a year now in between. He lived in a shack on the riverbank that had once belonged to his grandfather long time dead. On Tuesday and Friday he sold the fish he had caught that morning, the rest of the week he was drunk, loud, obscene, funny and outrageous. But he never touched anybody, never fought, never caressed. Once the people understood the boundaries and nature of his madness, they could fit him, so to speak, into the scheme of things.

Then, on subsequent National Suicide Days, the grown people looked out from behind curtains as he rang his bell; a few stragglers increased their speed, and little children screamed and ran! The tetter heads tried goading him (although he was only four or five years older than they) but not for long, for his curses were stingingly personal.

As time went along, the people took less notice of these January thirds, or rather they thought they did, thought they had no attitudes or feelings one way or another about Shadrack's annual solitary parade. In fact they had simply stopped remarking on the holiday because they had absorbed it into their thoughts, into their language, into their lives.

Someone said to a friend, "You sure was a long time delivering that baby. How long was you in labor?"

And the friend answered, " 'Bout three days. The pains started on Suicide Day and kept up till the following Sunday. Was borned on Sunday. All my boys is Sunday boys."

Some lover said to his bride-to-be, "Let's do it after New Years, 'stead of before. I get paid New Year's Eve."

And his sweetheart answered, "OK, but make sure it ain't on Suicide Day. I ain't 'bout to be listening to no cowbells whilst the weddin's going on."

Somebody's grandmother said her hens

always started a laying of double yolks right after Suicide Day.

Then Reverend Deal took it up, saying the same folks who had sense enough to avoid Shadrack's call were the ones who insisted on drinking themselves to death or womanizing themselves to death. "May's well go on with Shad and save the Lamb the trouble of redemption."

Easily, quietly, Suicide Day became a part of the fabric of life up in the Bottom of Medallion, Ohio.

1920

It had to be as far away from the Sundown House as possible. And her grandmother's middle-aged nephew who lived in a Northern town called Medallion was the one chance she had to make sure it would be. The red shutters had haunted both Helene Sabat and her grandmother for sixteen years. Helene was born behind those shutters, daughter of a Creole whore who worked there. The grandmother took Helene away from the soft lights and flowered carpets of the Sundown House and raised her under the dolesome eyes of a multicolored Virgin Mary, counseling her to be constantly on guard for any sign of her mother's wild blood.

So when Wiley Wright came to visit his Great Aunt Cecile in New Orleans, his enchantment with the pretty Helene became a marriage proposal — under the pressure of both women. He was a seaman (or rather a lakeman, for he was a ship's cook on one of the Great Lakes lines), in port only three days out of every sixteen.

He took his bride to his home in Medallion and put her in a lovely house with a brick porch and real lace curtains at the window. His long absences were quite bearable for Helene Wright, especially when, after some nine years of marriage, her daughter was born.

Her daughter was more comfort and purpose than she had ever hoped to find in this life. She rose grandly to the occasion of motherhood — grateful, deep down in her heart, that the child had not inherited the great beauty that was hers: that her skin had dusk in it, that her lashes were substantial but not undignified in their length, that she had taken the broad flat nose of Wiley (although Helene expected to improve it somewhat) and his generous lips.

Under Helene's hand the girl became obedient and polite. Any enthusiasms that little Nel showed were calmed by the mother until she drove her daughter's imagination underground.

Helene Wright was an impressive woman, at least in Medallion she was. Heavy hair in a bun, dark eyes arched in a perpetual query about other people's manners. A woman who won all social battles with presence and a conviction of the legitimacy of her authority. Since there was no Catholic church in Medallion then, she joined the most conservative black church. And held sway. It was Helene who never turned her head in church when latecomers arrived; Helene who established the practice of seasonal altar flowers; Helene who introduced the giving of banquets of welcome to returning Negro veterans. She lost only one battle — the pronunciation of her name. The people in the Bottom refused to say Helene. They called her Helen Wright and left it at that.

All in all her life was a satisfactory one. She loved her house and enjoyed manipulating her daughter and her husband. She would sigh sometimes just before falling asleep, thinking that she had indeed come far enough away from the Sundown House.

So it was with extremely mixed emotions that she read a letter from Mr. Henri Martin describing the illness of her grandmother, and suggesting she come down right away. She didn't want to go, but could not bring herself to ignore the silent plea of the woman who had rescued her.

It was November. November, 1920. Even in Medallion there was a victorious swagger in the legs of white men and a dull-eyed excitement in the eyes of colored veterans.

Helene thought about the trip South with heavy misgiving but decided that she had the best protection: her manner and her bearing, to which she would add a beautiful dress. She bought some deep-brown wool and three-fourths of a yard of matching velvet. Out of this she made herself a heavy but elegant dress with velvet collar and pockets.

Nel watched her mother cutting the pattern from newspapers and moving her eyes rapidly from a magazine model to her own hands. She watched her turn up the kerosene lamp at sunset to sew far into the night.

The day they were ready, Helene cooked a smoked ham, left a note for her lake-bound husband, in case he docked early, and walked head high and arms stiff with luggage ahead of her daughter to the train depot.

It was a longer walk than she remembered, and they saw the train steaming up just as they turned the corner. They ran

along the track looking for the coach
pointed out to them by the colored porter.
Even at that they made a mistake. Helene
and her daughter entered a coach peopled
by some twenty white men and women.
Rather than go back and down the three
wooden steps again, Helene decided to
spare herself some embarrassment and
walk on through to the colored car. She
carried two pieces of luggage and a string
purse; her daughter carried a covered
basket of food.

As they opened the door marked
COLORED ONLY, they saw a white conductor coming toward them. It was a chilly
day but a light skim of sweat glistened on
the woman's face as she and the little girl
struggled to hold the door open, hang on
to their luggage and enter all at once. The
conductor let his eyes travel over the pale
yellow woman and then stuck his little
finger into his ear, jiggling it free of wax.
"What you think you doin', gal?"

Helene looked up at him.

So soon. So soon. She hadn't even
begun the trip back. Back to her grandmother's house in the city where the red
shutters glowed, and already she had been
called "gal." All the old vulnerabilities, all
the old fears of being somehow flawed

gathered in her stomach and made her hands tremble. She had heard only that one word; it dangled above her wide-brimmed hat, which had slipped, in her exertion, from its carefully leveled placement and was now tilted in a bit of a jaunt over her eye.

Thinking he wanted her tickets, she quickly dropped both the cowhide suitcase and the straw one in order to search for them in her purse. An eagerness to please and an apology for living met in her voice. "I have them. Right here somewhere, sir . . ."

The conductor looked at the bit of wax his fingernail had retrieved. "What was you doin' back in there? What was you doin' in that coach yonder?"

Helene licked her lips. "Oh . . . I . . ." Her glance moved beyond the white man's face to the passengers seated behind him. Four or five black faces were watching, two belonging to soldiers still in their shit-colored uniforms and peaked caps. She saw their closed faces, their locked eyes, and turned for compassion to the gray eyes of the conductor.

"We made a mistake, sir. You see, there wasn't no sign. We just got in the wrong car, that's all. Sir."

"We don't 'low no mistakes on this train. Now git your butt on in there."

He stood there staring at her until she realized that he wanted her to move aside. Pulling Nel by the arm, she pressed herself and her daughter into the foot space in front of a wooden seat. Then, for no earthly reason, at least no reason that anybody could understand, certainly no reason that Nel understood then or later, she smiled. Like a street pup that wags its tail at the very doorjamb of the butcher shop he has been kicked away from only moments before, Helene smiled. Smiled dazzlingly and coquettishly at the salmon-colored face of the conductor.

Nel looked away from the flash of pretty teeth to the other passengers. The two black soldiers, who had been watching the scene with what appeared to be indifference, now looked stricken. Behind Nel was the bright and blazing light of her mother's smile; before her the midnight eyes of the soldiers. She saw the muscles of their faces tighten, a movement under the skin from blood to marble. No change in the expression of the eyes, but a hard wetness that veiled them as they looked at the stretch of her mother's foolish smile.

As the door slammed on the conductor's

exit, Helene walked down the aisle to a seat. She looked about for a second to see whether any of the men would help her put the suitcases in the overhead rack. Not a man moved. Helene sat down, fussily, her back toward the men. Nel sat opposite, facing both her mother and the soldiers, neither of whom she could look at. She felt both pleased and ashamed to sense that these men, unlike her father, who worshiped his graceful, beautiful wife, were bubbling with a hatred for her mother that had not been there in the beginning but had been born with the dazzling smile. In the silence that preceded the train's heave, she looked deeply at the folds of her mother's dress. There in the fall of the heavy brown wool she held her eyes. She could not risk letting them travel upward for fear of seeing that the hooks and eyes in the placket of the dress had come undone and exposed the custard-colored skin underneath. She stared at the hem, wanting to believe in its weight but knowing that custard was all that it hid. If this tall, proud woman, this woman who was very particular about her friends, who slipped into church with unequaled elegance, who could quell a roustabout with a look, if *she* were really custard, then there was a chance that Nel was too.

It was on that train, shuffling toward Cincinnati, that she resolved to be on guard — always. She wanted to make certain that no man ever looked at her that way. That no midnight eyes or marbled flesh would ever accost her and turn her into jelly.

For two days they rode; two days of watching sleet turn to rain, turn to purple sunsets, and one night knotted on the wooden seats (their heads on folded coats), trying not to hear the snoring soldiers. When they changed trains in Birmingham for the last leg of the trip, they discovered what luxury they had been in through Kentucky and Tennessee, where the rest stops had all had colored toilets. After Birmingham there were none. Helene's face was drawn with the need to relieve herself, and so intense was her distress she finally brought herself to speak about her problem to a black woman with four children who had got on in Tuscaloosa.

"Is there somewhere we can go to use the restroom?"

The woman looked up at her and seemed not to understand. "Ma'am?" Her eyes fastened on the thick velvet collar, the fair skin, the high-tone voice.

"The restroom," Helene repeated. Then, in a whisper, "The toilet."

The woman pointed out the window and said, "Yes, ma'am. Yonder."

Helene looked out of the window halfway expecting to see a comfort station in the distance; instead she saw gray-green trees leaning over tangled grass. "Where?"

"Yonder," the woman said. "Meridian. We be pullin' in direc'lin." Then she smiled sympathetically and asked, "Kin you make it?"

Helene nodded and went back to her seat trying to think of other things — for the surest way to have an accident would be to remember her full bladder.

At Meridian the women got out with their children. While Helene looked about the tiny stationhouse for a door that said COLORED WOMEN, the other woman stalked off to a field of high grass on the far side of the track. Some white men were leaning on the railing in front of the stationhouse. It was not only their tongues curling around toothpicks that kept Helene from asking information of them. She looked around for the other woman and, seeing just the top of her head rag in the grass, slowly realized where "yonder" was. All of them, the fat woman and her four children, three boys and a girl, Helene and her daughter, squatted there in the four o'clock Meridian sun. They did it again in Ellisville, again in Hattiesburg, and by the time they reached Slidell, not too far from Lake Pontchartrain, Helene could not only fold leaves as well as the fat woman, she never felt a stir as she passed the muddy eyes of the men who stood like wrecked Dorics under the station roofs of those towns.

The lift in spirit that such an accomplishment produced in her quickly disappeared when the train finally pulled into New Orleans.

Cecile Sabat's house leaned between two others just like it on Elysian Fields. A Frenchified shotgun house, it sported a magnificent garden in the back and a tiny wrought-iron fence in the front. On the door hung a black crepe wreath with purple ribbon. They were too late. Helene reached up to touch the ribbon, hesitated, and knocked. A man in a collarless shirt opened the door. Helene identified herself and he said he was Henri Martin and that he was there for the settin'-up. They stepped into the house. The Virgin Mary clasped her hands in front of her neck three times in the front room and once in the bedroom where Cecile's body lay. The old woman had died without seeing or blessing her granddaughter.

No one other than Mr. Martin seemed to be in the house, but a sweet odor as of gardenias told them that someone else had been. Blotting her lashes with a white handkerchief, Helene walked through the kitchen to the back bedroom where she had slept for sixteen years. Nel trotted along behind, enchanted with the smell, the candles and the strangeness. When Helene bent to loosen the ribbons of Nel's hat, a woman in a yellow dress came out of the garden and onto the back porch that opened into the bedroom. The two women looked at each other. There was no recognition in the eyes of either. Then Helene said, "This is your . . . grandmother, Nel." Nel looked at her mother and then quickly back at the door they had just come out of.

"No. That was your great-grandmother. This is your grandmother. My . . . mother."

Before the child could think, her words were hanging in the gardenia air. "But she looks so young."

The woman in the canary-yellow dress

laughed and said she was forty-eight, "an old forty-eight."

Then it was she who carried the gardenia smell. This tiny woman with the softness and glare of a canary. In that somber house that held four Virgin Marys, where death sighed in every corner and candles sputtered, the gardenia smell and canary-yellow dress emphasized the funeral atmosphere surrounding them.

The woman smiled, glanced in the mirror and said, throwing her voice toward Helene, "That your only one?"

"Yes," said Helene.

"Pretty. A lot like you."

"Yes. Well. She's ten now."

"Ten? Vrai? Small for her age, no?"

Helene shrugged and looked at her daughter's questioning eyes. The woman in the yellow dress leaned forward. "Come. Come, chere."

Helene interrupted. "We have to get cleaned up. We been three days on the train with no chance to wash or . . ."

"Comment t'appelle?"

"She doesn't talk Creole."

"Then you ask her."

"She wants to know your name, honey."

With her head pressed into her mother's heavy brown dress, Nel told her and then asked, "What's yours?"

"Mine's Rochelle. Well. I must be going on." She moved closer to the mirror and stood there sweeping hair up from her neck back into its halo-like roll, and wetting with spit the ringlets that fell over her ears. "I been here, you know, most of the day. She pass on yesterday. The funeral tomorrow. Henri takin' care." She struck a match, blew it out and darkened her eyebrows with the burnt head. All the while Helene and Nel watched her. The one in a rage at the folded leaves she had endured, the wooden benches she had slept on, all to miss seeing her grandmother and seeing instead that painted canary who never said a word of greeting or affection or . . .

Rochelle continued. "I don't know what happen to de house. Long time paid for. You be thinkin' on it? Oui?" Her newly darkened eyebrows queried Helene.

"Oui." Helene's voice was chilly. "I be thinkin' on it."

"Oh, well. Not for me to say . . ."

Suddenly she swept around and hugged Nel — a quick embrace tighter and harder than one would have imagined her thin soft arms capable of.

" 'Voir! 'Voir!" and she was gone.

In the kitchen, being soaped head to toe

41

by her mother, Nel ventured an observation. "She smelled so nice. And her skin was so soft."

Helene rinsed the cloth. "Much handled things are always soft."

"What does 'vwah' mean?"

"I don't know," her mother said. "I don't talk Creole." She gazed at her daughter's wet buttocks. "And neither do you."

When they got back to Medallion and into the quiet house they saw the note exactly where they had left it and the ham dried out in the icebox.

"Lord, I've never been so glad to see this place. But look at the dust. Get the rags, Nel. Oh, never mind. Let's breathe awhile first. Lord, I never thought I'd get back here safe and sound. Whoo. Well, it's over. Good and over. Praise His name. Look at that. I told that old fool not to deliver any milk and there's the can curdled to beat all. What gets into people? I told him not to. Well, I got other things to worry 'bout. Got to get a fire started. I left it ready so I wouldn't have to do nothin' but light it. Lord, it's cold. Don't just sit there, honey. You could be pulling your nose . . ."

Nel sat on the red-velvet sofa listening to her mother but remembering the smell and

42

the tight, tight hug of the woman in yellow who rubbed burned matches over her eyes.

Late that night after the fire was made, the cold supper eaten, the surface dust removed, Nel lay in bed thinking of her trip. She remembered clearly the urine running down and into her stockings until she learned how to squat properly; the disgust on the face of the dead woman and the sound of the funeral drums. It had been an exhilarating trip but a fearful one. She had been frightened of the soldiers' eyes on the train, the black wreath on the door, the custard pudding she believed lurked under her mother's heavy dress, the feel of unknown streets. and unknown people. But she had gone on a real trip, and now she was different. She got out of bed and lit the lamp to look in the mirror. There was her face, plain brown eyes, three braids and the nose her mother hated. She looked for a long time and suddenly a shiver ran through her.

"I'm me," she whispered. "Me."

Nel didn't know quite what she meant, but on the other hand she knew exactly what she meant.

"I'm me. I'm not their daughter. I'm not Nel. I'm me. Me."

Each time she said the word *me* there

was a gathering in her like power, like joy, like fear. Back in bed with her discovery, she stared out the window at the dark leaves of the horse chestnut.

"Me," she murmured. And then, sinking deeper into the quilts, "I want . . . I want to be . . . wonderful. Oh, Jesus, make me wonderful."

The many experiences of her trip crowded in on her. She slept. It was the last as well as the first time she was ever to leave Medallion.

For days afterward she imagined other trips she would take, alone though, to far-away places. Contemplating them was delicious. Leaving Medallion would be her goal. But that was before she met Sula, the girl she had seen for five years at Garfield Primary but never played with, never knew, because her mother said that Sula's mother was sooty. The trip, perhaps, or her new found me-ness, gave her the strength to cultivate a friend in spite of her mother.

When Sula first visited the Wright house, Helene's curdled scorn turned to butter. Her daughter's friend seemed to have none of the mother's slackness. Nel, who regarded the oppressive neatness of her home with dread, felt comfortable in it with Sula, who loved it and would sit on the red-velvet sofa for ten to twenty minutes at a time — still as dawn. As for Nel, she preferred Sula's woolly house, where a pot of something was always cooking on the stove; where the mother, Hannah, never scolded or gave directions; where all sorts of people dropped in; where newspapers were stacked in the hallway, and dirty dishes left for hours at a time in the sink, and where a one-legged grandmother named Eva handed you goobers from deep inside her pockets or read you a dream.

1921

Sula Peace lived in a house of many rooms that had been built over a period of five years to the specifications of its owner, who kept on adding things: more stairways — there were three sets to the second floor — more rooms, doors and stoops. There were rooms that had three doors, others that opened out on the porch only and were inaccessible from any other part of the house; others that you could get to only by going through somebody's bedroom. The creator and sovereign of this enormous house with the four sickle-pear trees in the front yard and the single elm in the back yard was Eva Peace, who sat in a wagon on the third floor directing the lives of her children, friends, strays, and a constant stream of boarders. Fewer than nine people in the town remembered when Eva had two legs, and her oldest child, Hannah, was not one of them. Unless Eva herself introduced the subject, no one ever spoke of her disability; they pretended to ignore it, unless, in some mood of fancy, she began some fearful story about it — generally to entertain children. How the leg got up by itself one day and walked on off. How she hobbled after it but it ran too fast. Or how she had a corn on her toe and it just grew and grew and grew until her whole foot was a corn and then it traveled on up her leg and wouldn't stop growing until she put a red rag at the top but by that time it was already at her knee.

Somebody said Eva stuck it under a train and made them pay off. Another said she sold it to a hospital for $10,000 — at which Mr. Reed opened his eyes and asked, "Nigger gal legs goin' for $10,000 a *piece?*" as though he could understand $10,000 a *pair* — but for *one?*

Whatever the fate of her lost leg, the remaining one was magnificent. It was stockinged and shod at all times and in all weather. Once in a while she got a felt slipper for Christmas or her birthday, but they soon disappeared, for Eva always wore a black laced-up shoe that came well above her ankle. Nor did she wear overlong dresses to disguise the empty place on her left side. Her dresses were mid-calf so that her one glamorous leg was always in view as well as the long fall of space below her left thigh. One of her men friends had fashioned a kind of wheelchair for her: a rocking-chair top fitted into a large child's wagon. In this contraption she wheeled around the room, from bedside to dresser to the balcony that opened out the north side of her room or to the window that looked out on the back yard. The wagon was so low that children who spoke to her standing up were eye level with her, and adults, standing or sitting, had to look down at her. But they didn't know it. They all had the impression that they were looking up at her, up into the open distances of her eyes, up into the soft black of her nostrils and up at the crest of her chin.

Eva had married a man named BoyBoy and had three children: Hannah, the eldest, and Eva, whom she named after herself but called Pearl, and a son named Ralph, whom she called Plum.

After five years of a sad and disgruntled marriage BoyBoy took off. During the time they were together he was very much preoccupied with other women and not home much. He did whatever he could that he liked, and he liked womanizing best, drinking second, and abusing Eva third. When he left in November, Eva had $1.65, five eggs, three beets and no idea of what or how to feel. The children needed her; she needed money, and needed to get on with her life. But the demands of feeding her three children were so acute she had to postpone her anger for two years until she had both the time and the energy for it. She was confused and desperately hungry. There were very few black families in those low hills then. The Suggs, who lived two hundred yards down the road, brought her a warm bowl of peas, as soon as they found out, and a plate of cold bread. She thanked them and asked if they had a little milk for the older ones. They said no, but Mrs. Jackson, they knew, had a cow still giving. Eva took a bucket over and Mrs. Jackson told her to come back and fill it up in the morning, because the evening milking had already been done. In this way, things went on until near December. People were very willing to help, but Eva felt she would soon run her welcome out; winters were hard and her neighbors were not that much better off. She would lie in bed with the baby boy, the two girls wrapped in quilts on the floor, thinking. The oldest child, Hannah, was five and too young to take care of the baby alone, and any housework Eva could find would keep her away from them from five thirty or earlier in the morning until dark — way past eight. The white people in the valley weren't rich enough then to want maids; they were small farmers and tradesmen and wanted hard-labor help if anything. She thought also of returning to some of her people in Virginia, but to come home dragging three young ones would have to be a step one rung before death for Eva. She would have to scrounge around and beg through the winter, until her baby was at least nine months old, then she could plant and maybe hire herself out to valley farms to weed or sow or feed stock until something steadier came along at harvest time. She thought she had probably been a fool to let BoyBoy haul her away from her people, but it had seemed so right at the time. He worked for a white carpenter and toolsmith who insisted on BoyBoy's accompanying him when he went West and set up in a squinchy little town called Medallion. BoyBoy brought his new wife and built them a one-room cabin sixty feet back from the road that wound up out of the valley, on up into the hills and was named for the man he worked for. They lived there a year before they had an outhouse.

Sometime before the middle of December, the baby, Plum, stopped having bowel movements. Eva massaged his stomach and gave him warm water. Something must be wrong with my milk, she thought. Mrs. Suggs gave her castor oil, but even that didn't work. He cried and fought so they couldn't get much down his throat anyway. He seemed in great pain and his shrieks were pitched high in outrage and suffering. At one point, maddened by his own crying, he gagged, choked and looked as though he was strangling to death. Eva rushed to him and kicked over the earthen slop jar, washing a small area of the floor with the child's urine. She managed to soothe him, but when he took up the cry again late that night, she resolved to end his misery once and for all. She wrapped him in blankets, ran her finger around the crevices and sides of the lard can and stumbled to the outhouse with him. Deep in its darkness and freezing stench she squatted down, turned the baby over on her knees, exposed his buttocks and shoved the last bit of food she had in the world (besides three beets) up his ass. Softening the insertion with the dab of lard, she probed with her middle finger to loosen his bowels. Her fingernail snagged what felt like a pebble; she pulled it out and others followed. Plum stopped crying as the black hard stools ricocheted onto the frozen ground. And now that it was over, Eva squatted there wondering why she had come all the way out there to free his stools, and what was she doing down on her haunches with her beloved baby boy warmed by her body in the almost total darkness, her shins and teeth freezing, her nostrils assailed. She shook her head as though to juggle her brains around, then said aloud, "Uh uh. Nooo." Thereupon she returned to the house and her bed. As the grateful Plum slept, the silence allowed her to think.

Two days later she left all of her children with Mrs. Suggs, saying she would be back the next day.

Eighteen months later she swept down from a wagon with two crutches, a new black pocketbook, and one leg. First she reclaimed her children, next she gave the surprised Mrs. Suggs a ten-dollar bill, later she started building a house on Carpenter's Road, sixty feet from BoyBoy's one-room cabin, which she rented out.

When Plum was three years old, BoyBoy came back to town and paid her a visit.

When Eva got the word that he was on his way, she made some lemonade. She had no idea what she would do or feel during that encounter. Would she cry, cut his throat, beg him to make love to her? She couldn't imagine. So she just waited to see. She stirred lemonade in a green pitcher and waited.

BoyBoy danced up the steps and knocked on the door.

"Come on in," she hollered.

He opened the door and stood smiling, a picture of prosperity and good will. His shoes were a shiny orange, and he had on a citified straw hat, a light-blue suit, and a cat's-head stickpin in his tie. Eva smiled and told him to sit himself down. He smiled too.

"How you been, girl?"

"Pretty fair. What you know good?" When she heard those words come out of her own mouth she knew that their conversation would start off polite. Although it remained to be seen whether she would still run the ice pick through the cat's-head pin.

"Have some lemonade."

"Don't mind if I do." He swept his hat off with a satisfied gesture. His nails were long and shiny. "Sho is hot, and I been runnin' around all day."

Eva looked out of the screen door and saw a woman in a pea-green dress leaning on the smallest pear tree. Glancing back at him, she was reminded of Plum's face when he managed to get the meat out of a walnut all by himself. Eva smiled again, and poured the lemonade.

Their conversation was easy: she catching him up on all the gossip, he asking about this one and that one, and like everybody else avoiding any reference to her leg. It was like talking to somebody's cousin who just stopped by to say howdy before getting on back to wherever he came from. BoyBoy didn't ask to see the children, and Eva didn't bring them into the conversation.

After a while he rose to go. Talking about his appointments and exuding an odor of new money and idleness, he danced down the steps and strutted toward the pea-green dress. Eva watched. She looked at the back of his neck and the set of his shoulders. Underneath all of that shine she saw defeat in the stalk of his neck and the curious tight way he held his shoulders. But still she was not sure what she felt. Then he leaned forward and whispered into the ear of the woman in the green dress. She was still for a moment and then threw back her head and laughed. A high-pitched big-city laugh that reminded Eva of Chicago. It hit her like a sledge hammer, and it was then that she knew what to feel. A liquid trail of hate flooded her chest.

Knowing that she would hate him long and well filled her with pleasant anticipation, like when you know you are going to fall in love with someone and you wait for the happy signs. Hating BoyBoy, she could get on with it, and have the safety, the thrill, the consistency of that hatred as long as she wanted or needed it to define and strengthen her or protect her from routine vulnerabilities. (Once when Hannah accused her of hating colored people, Eva said she only hated one, Hannah's father BoyBoy, and it was hating him that kept her alive and happy.)

Happy or not, after BoyBoy's visit she began her retreat to her bedroom, leaving the bottom of the house more and more to those who lived there: cousins who were passing through, stray folks, and the many, many newly married couples she let rooms to with housekeeping privileges, and after 1910 she didn't willingly set foot on the stairs but once and that was to light a fire, the smoke of which was in her hair for years.

Among the tenants in that big old house were the children Eva took in. Operating on a private scheme of preference and prejudice, she sent off for children she had seen from the balcony of her bedroom or whose circumstances she had heard about from the gossipy old men who came to play checkers or read the *Courier*, or write her number. In 1921, when her granddaughter Sula was eleven, Eva had three such children. They came with woolen caps and names given to them by their mothers, or grandmothers, or somebody's best friend. Eva snatched the caps off their heads and ignored their names. She looked at the first child closely, his wrists, the shape of his head and the temperament that showed in his eyes and said, "Well. Look at Dewey. My my mymymy." When later that same year she sent for a child who kept falling down off the porch across the street, she said the same thing. Somebody said, "But, Miss Eva, you calls the other one Dewey."

"So? This here's another one."

When the third one was brought and Eva said "Dewey" again, everybody thought she had simply run out of names or that her faculties had finally softened.

"How is anybody going to tell them apart?" Hannah asked her.

"What you need to tell them apart for? They's all deweys."

When Hannah asked the question it didn't sound very bright, because each dewey was markedly different from the other two. Dewey one was a deeply black boy with a beautiful head and the golden eyes of chronic jaundice. Dewey two was light-skinned with freckles everywhere and a head of tight red hair. Dewey three was half Mexican with chocolate skin and black bangs. Besides, they were one and two years apart in age. It was Eva saying things like, "Send one of them deweys out to get me some Garret, if they don't have Garret, get Buttercup," or, "Tell them deweys to cut out that noise," or, "Come here, you dewey you," and, "Send me a dewey," that gave Hannah's question its weight.

Slowly each boy came out of whatever cocoon he was in at the time his mother or somebody gave him away, and accepted Eva's view, becoming in fact as well as in name a dewey — joining with the other two to become a trinity with a plural name . . . inseparable, loving nothing and no one but themselves. When the handle from the icebox fell off, all the deweys got whipped, and in dry-eyed silence watched their own feet as they turned their behinds high up into the air for the stroke. When the golden-eyed dewey was ready for school he would not go without the others. He was seven, freckled dewey was five, and Mexican dewey was only four. Eva solved the problem by having them all sent off together. Mr. Buckland Reed said, "But one of them's only four."

"How you know? They all come here the same year," Eva said.

"But that one there was one year old when he came, and that was three years ago."

"You don't know how old he was when he come here and neither do the teacher. Send 'em."

The teacher was startled but not unbelieving, for she had long ago given up trying to fathom the ways of the colored people in town. So when Mrs. Reed said that their names were Dewey King, that they were cousins, and all were six years old, the teacher gave only a tiny sigh and wrote them in the record book for the first grade. She too thought she would have no problem distinguishing among them, because they looked nothing alike, but like everyone else before her, she gradually found that she could not tell one from the other. The deweys would not allow it. They got all mixed up in her head, and finally she could not literally believe her eyes. They spoke with one voice, thought with one mind, and maintained an annoying privacy. Stouthearted, surly, and wholly unpredictable, the deweys remained a mystery not only during all of their lives in Medallion but after as well.

The deweys came in 1921, but the year before Eva had given a small room off the kitchen to Tar Baby, a beautiful, slight, quiet man who never spoke above a whisper. Most people said he was half white, but Eva said he was all white. That she knew blood when she saw it, and he didn't have none. When he first came to Medallion, the people called him Pretty Johnnie, but Eva looked at his milky skin and cornsilk hair and out of a mixture of fun and meanness called him Tar Baby. He was a mountain boy who stayed to himself, bothering no one, intent solely on drinking himself to death. At first he worked in a poultry market, and after wringing the necks of chickens all day, he came home and drank until he slept. Later he began to miss days at work and frequently did not have his rent money. When he lost his job altogether, he would go out in the morning, scrounge around for money doing odd jobs, bumming or whatever, and come home to drink. Because he was no bother, ate little, required nothing, and was a lover of cheap wine, no one found him a nuisance. Besides, he frequently went to Wednesday-night prayer meetings and sang with the sweetest hill voice imaginable "In the Sweet By-and-By." He sent the deweys out for his liquor and spent most of his time in a heap on the floor or sitting in a chair staring at the wall.

Hannah worried about him a little, but only a very little. For it soon became clear that he simply wanted a place to die privately but not quite alone. No one thought of suggesting to him that he pull himself together or see a doctor or anything. Even the women at prayer meeting who cried when he sang "In the Sweet By-and-By" never tried to get him to participate in the church activities. They just listened to him sing, wept and thought very graphically of their own imminent deaths. The people either accepted his own evaluation of his life, or were indifferent to it. There was, however, a measure of contempt in their indifference, for they had little patience with people who took themselves that seriously. Seriously enough to try to die. And it was natural that he, after all, became the first one to join Shadrack — Tar Baby and the deweys — on National Suicide Day.

Under Eva's distant eye, and prey to her idiosyncrasies, her own children grew up stealthily: Pearl married at fourteen and moved to Flint, Michigan, from where she posted frail letters to her mother with two dollars folded into the writing paper. Sad little nonsense letters about minor troubles, her husband's job and who the children favored. Hannah married a laughing man named Rekus who died when their daughter Sula was about three years old, at which time Hannah moved back into her mother's big house prepared to take care of it and her mother forever.

With the exception of BoyBoy, those Peace women loved all men. It was man-love that Eva bequeathed to her daughters. Probably, people said, because there were no men in the house, no men to run it. But actually that was not true. The Peace women simply loved maleness, for its own sake. Eva, old as she was, and with one leg, had a regular flock of gentleman callers, and although she did not participate in the act of love, there was a good deal of teasing and pecking and laughter. The men wanted to see her lovely calf, that neat shoe, and watch the focusing that sometimes swept down out of the distances in her eyes. They wanted to see the joy in her face as they settled down to play checkers, knowing that even when she beat them, as she almost always did, somehow, in her presence, it was they who had won something. They would read the newspaper aloud to her and make observations on its content, and Eva would listen feeling no obligation to agree and, in fact, would take them to task about their interpretation of events. But she argued with them with such an absence of bile, such a concentration of manlove, that they felt their convictions solidified by her disagreement.

With other people's affairs Eva was equally prejudiced about men. She fussed interminably with the brides of the newly wed couples for not getting their men's supper ready on time; about how to launder shirts, press them, etc. "Yo' man be here direc'lin. Ain't it 'bout time you got busy?"

"Aw, Miss Eva. It'll be ready. We just having spaghetti."

"Again?" Eva's eyebrows fluted up and the newlywed pressed her lips together in shame.

Hannah simply refused to live without the attentions of a man, and after Rekus' death had a steady sequence of lovers, mostly the husbands of her friends and neighbors. Her flirting was sweet, low and guileless. Without ever a pat of the hair, a rush to change clothes or a quick application of paint, with no gesture whatsoever, she rippled with sex. In her same old print wraparound, barefoot in the summer, in the winter her feet in a man's leather slippers with the backs flattened under her heels, she made men aware of her behind, her slim ankles, the dew-smooth skin and the incredible length of neck. Then the smile-eyes, the turn of the head — all so welcoming, light and playful. Her voice trailed, dipped and bowed; she gave a chord to the simplest words. Nobody, but nobody, could say "hey sugar" like Hannah. When he heard it, the man tipped his hat down a little over his eyes, hoisted his trousers and thought about the hollow place at the base of her neck. And all this without the slightest confusion about work and responsibilities. While Eva tested and argued with her men, leaving them feeling as though they had been in combat with a worthy, if amiable, foe, Hannah rubbed no edges, made no demands, made the man feel as though he were complete and wonderful just as he was — he didn't need fixing — and so he relaxed and swooned in the Hannah-light that shone on him simply because he was. If the man entered and Hannah was carrying a coal scuttle up from the basement, she handled it in such a way that it became a gesture of love. He made no move to help her with it simply because he wanted to see how her thighs looked when she bent to put it down, knowing that she wanted him to see them too.

But since in that crowded house there were no places for private and spontaneous lovemaking, Hannah would take the man down into the cellar in the summer where it was cool back behind the coal bin and the newspapers, or in the winter they would step into the pantry and stand up against the shelves she had filled with canned goods, or lie on the flour sack just under the rows of tiny green peppers. When those places were not available, she would slip into the seldom-used parlor, or even up to her bedroom. She liked the last place least, not because Sula slept in the room with her but because her love mate's tendency was always to fall asleep afterward and Hannah was fastidious about whom she slept with. She would fuck practically anything, but sleeping with someone implied for her a measure of trust and a definite commitment. So she ended up a daylight lover, and it was only once actually that Sula came home from school and found her mother in the bed, curled spoon in the arms of a man.

Seeing her step so easily into the pantry and emerge looking precisely as she did when she entered, only happier, taught Sula that sex was pleasant and frequent, but otherwise unremarkable. Outside the house, where children giggled about underwear, the message was different. So she watched her mother's face and the face of the men when they opened the pantry door and made up her own mind.

Hannah exasperated the women in the town — the "good" women, who said, "One thing I can't stand is a nasty woman"; the whores, who were hard put to find trade among black men anyway and who resented Hannah's generosity; the middling women, who had both husbands and affairs, because Hannah seemed too unlike them, having no passion attached to her relationships and being wholly incapable of jealousy. Hannah's friendships with women were, of course, seldom and short-lived, and the newly married couples whom her mother took in soon learned what a hazard she was. She could break up a marriage before it had even become one — she would make love to the new groom and wash his wife's dishes all in an afternoon. What she wanted, after Rekus died, and what she succeeded in having more often than not, was some touching every day.

The men, surprisingly, never gossiped about her. She was unquestionably a kind and generous woman and that, coupled with her extraordinary beauty and funky elegance of manner, made them defend her and protect her from any vitriol that newcomers or their wives might spill.

Eva's last child, Plum, to whom she hoped to bequeath everything, floated in a constant swaddle of love and affection, until 1917 when he went to war. He returned to the States in 1919 but did not get back to Medallion until 1920. He wrote letters from New York, Washington, D.C., and Chicago full of promises of homecomings, but there was obviously something wrong. Finally some two or three days after Christmas, he arrived with just the shadow of his old dip-down walk. His hair had been neither cut nor combed in months, his clothes were pointless and he had no socks. But he did have a black bag, a paper sack, and a sweet, sweet smile. Everybody welcomed him and gave him a warm room next to Tar Baby's and waited for him to tell them whatever it was he wanted them to know. They waited in vain for his telling but not long for the knowing. His habits were much like Tar Baby's but there were no bottles, and Plum was sometimes cheerful and animated. Hannah watched and Eva waited. Then he began to steal from them, take trips to Cincinnati and sleep for days in his room with the record player going. He got even thinner, since he ate only snatches of things at beginnings or endings of meals. It was Hannah who found the bent spoon black from steady cooking.

So late one night in 1921, Eva got up from her bed and put on her clothes. Hoisting herself up on her crutches, she was amazed to find that she could still manage them, although the pain in her armpits was severe. She practiced a few steps around the room, and then opened the door. Slowly, she manipulated herself down the long flights of stairs, two crutches under her left arm, the right hand grasping the banister. The sound of her foot booming in comparison to the delicate pat of the crutch tip. On each landing she stopped for breath. Annoyed at her physical condition, she closed her eyes and removed the crutches from under her arms to relieve the unaccustomed pressure. At the foot of the stairs she redistributed her weight between the crutches and swooped on through the front room, to the dining room, to the kitchen, swinging and swooping like a giant heron, so graceful sailing about in its own habitat but awkward and comical when it folded its wings and tried to walk. With a swing and a swoop she arrived at Plum's door and pushed it open with the tip of one crutch. He was lying in bed barely visible in the light coming from a single bulb. Eva swung over to the bed and propped her crutches at its foot. She sat down and gathered Plum into her arms. He woke, but only slightly.

"Hey, man. Hey. You holdin' me, Mamma?" His voice was drowsy and amused. He chuckled as though he had heard some private joke. Eva held him closer and began to rock. Back and forth she rocked him, her eyes wandering around his room. There in the corner was a half-eaten store-bought cherry pie. Balled-up candy wrappers and empty pop bottles peeped from under the dresser. On the floor by her foot was a glass of strawberry crush and a *Liberty* magazine. Rocking, rocking, listening to Plum's occasional chuckles, Eva let her memory spin, loop and fall. Plum in the tub that time as she leaned over him. He reached up and dripped water into her bosom and laughed. She was angry, but not too, and laughed with him.

"Mamma, you so purty. You so purty, Mamma."

Eva lifted her tongue to the edge of her lip to stop the tears from running into her mouth. Rocking, rocking. Later she laid him down and looked at him a long time. Suddenly she was thirsty and reached for the glass of strawberry crush. She put it to her lips and discovered it was blood-tainted water and threw it to the floor. Plum woke up and said, "Hey, Mamma, whyn't you go on back to bed? I'm all right. Didn't I tell you? I'm all right. Go on, now."

"I'm going, Plum," she said. She shifted her weight and pulled her crutches toward her. Swinging and swooping, she left his room. She dragged herself to the kitchen and made grating noises.

Plum on the rim of a warm light sleep was still chuckling. Mamma. She sure was somethin'. He felt twilight. Now there seemed to be some kind of wet light traveling over his legs and stomach with a deeply attractive smell. It wound itself — this wet light — all about him, splashing and running into his skin. He opened his eyes and saw what he imagined was the great wing of an eagle pouring a wet lightness over him. Some kind of baptism, some kind of blessing, he thought. Everything is going to be all right, it said. Knowing that it was so he closed his eyes and sank back into the bright hole of sleep.

Eva stepped back from the bed and let the crutches rest under her arms. She rolled a bit of newspaper into a tight stick about six inches long, lit it and threw it onto the bed where the kerosene-soaked Plum lay in snug delight. Quickly, as the *whoosh* of flames engulfed him, she shut the door and made her slow and painful journey back to the top of the house.

Just as she got to the third landing she could hear Hannah and some child's voice. She swung along, not even listening to the voices of alarm and the cries of the deweys. By the time she got to her bed someone was bounding up the stairs after her. Hannah opened the door. "Plum! Plum! He's burning, Mamma! We can't even open the door! Mamma!"

Eva looked into Hannah's eyes. "Is? My baby? Burning?" The two women did not speak, for the eyes of each were enough for the other. Then Hannah closed hers and ran toward the voices of neighbors calling for water.

1922

It was too cool for ice cream. A hill wind was blowing dust and empty Camels wrappers about their ankles. It pushed their dresses into the creases of their behinds, then lifted the hems to peek at their cotton underwear. They were on their way to Edna Finch's Mellow House, an ice-cream parlor catering to nice folks — where even children would feel comfortable, you know, even though it was right next to Reba's Grill and just one block down from the Time and a Half Pool Hall. It sat in the curve of Carpenter's Road, which, in four blocks, made up all the sporting life available in the Bottom. Old men and young ones draped themselves in front of the Elmira Theater, Irene's Palace of Cosmetology, the pool hall, the grill and the other sagging business enterprises that lined the street. On sills, on stoops, on crates and broken chairs they sat tasting their teeth and waiting for something to distract them.

Every passerby, every motorcar, every alteration in stance caught their attention and was commented on. Particularly they watched women. When a woman approached, the older men tipped their hats; the younger ones opened and closed their thighs. But all of them, whatever their age, watched her retreating view with interest.

Nel and Sula walked through this valley of eyes chilled by the wind and heated by the embarrassment of appraising stares. The old men looked at their stalklike legs, dwelled on the cords in the backs of their knees and remembered old dance steps they had not done in twenty years. In their lust, which age had turned to kindness, they moved their lips as though to stir up the taste of young sweat on tight skin.

Pig meat. The words were in all their minds. And one of them, one of the young ones, said it aloud. Softly but definitively and there was no mistaking the compliment. His name was Ajax, a twenty-one-year-old pool haunt of sinister beauty. Graceful and economical in every movement, he held a place of envy with men of all ages for his magnificently foul mouth. In fact he seldom cursed, and the epithets he chose were dull, even harmless. His reputation was derived from the way he handled the words. When he said "hell" he hit the *h* with his lungs and the impact was greater than the achievement of the most imaginative foul mouth in the town. He could say "shit" with a nastiness impossible to imitate. So, when he said "pig meat" as Nel and Sula passed, they guarded their eyes lest someone see their delight.

It was not really Edna Finch's ice cream that made them brave the stretch of those panther eyes. Years later their own eyes would glaze as they cupped their chins in remembrance of the inchworm smiles, the squatting haunches, the track-rail legs straddling broken chairs. The cream-colored trousers marking with a mere seam the place where the mystery curled. Those smooth vanilla crotches invited them; those lemon-yellow gabardines beckoned to them.

They moved toward the ice-cream parlor like tightrope walkers, as thrilled by the possibility of a slip as by the maintenance of tension and balance. The least sideways glance, the merest toe stub, could pitch them into those creamy haunches spread wide with welcome. Somewhere beneath all of that daintiness, chambered in all that neatness, lay the thing that clotted their dreams.

Which was only fitting, for it was in dreams that the two girls had first met. Long before Edna Finch's Mellow House opened, even before they marched through the chocolate halls of Garfield Primary School out onto the playground and stood facing each other through the ropes of the one vacant swing ("Go on." "No. You go."), they had already made each other's acquaintance in the delirium of their noon dreams. They were solitary little girls whose loneliness was so profound it intoxicated them and sent them stumbling into Technicolored visions that always included a presence, a someone, who, quite like the dreamer, shared the delight of the dream. When Nel, an only child, sat on the steps of her back porch surrounded by the high silence of her mother's incredibly orderly house, feeling the neatness pointing at her back, she studied the poplars and fell easily into a picture of herself lying on a flowered bed, tangled in her own hair, waiting for some fiery prince. He approached but never quite arrived. But always, watching the dream along with her, were some smiling sympathetic eyes. Someone as interested as she herself in the flow of her imagined hair, the thickness of the mattress of flowers, the voile sleeves that closed below her elbows in gold-threaded cuffs.

Similarly, Sula, also an only child, but wedged into a household of throbbing disorder constantly awry with things, people, voices and the slamming of doors, spent hours in the attic behind a roll of linoleum galloping through her own mind on a gray-and-white horse tasting sugar and smelling roses in full view of a someone who shared both the taste and the speed.

So when they met, first in those chocolate halls and next through the ropes of the swing, they felt the ease and comfort of old friends. Because each had discovered years before that they were neither white nor male, and that all freedom and triumph was forbidden to them, they had set about creating something else to be. Their meeting was fortunate, for it let them use each other to grow on. Daughters of distant mothers and incomprehensible fathers (Sula's because he was dead; Nel's because he wasn't), they found in each other's eyes the intimacy they were looking for.

Nel Wright and Sula Peace were both twelve in 1922, wishbone thin and easy-assed. Nel was the color of wet sandpaper — just dark enough to escape the blows of the pitch-black truebloods and the contempt of old women who worried about such things as bad blood mixtures and knew that the origins of a mule and a mulatto were one and the same. Had she been any lighter-skinned she would have needed either her mother's protection on the way to school or a streak of mean to defend herself. Sula was a heavy brown with large quiet eyes, one of which featured a birthmark that spread from the middle of the lid toward the eyebrow, shaped something like a stemmed rose. It gave her otherwise plain face a broken excitement and blueblade threat like the keloid scar of the razored man who sometimes played checkers with her grandmother. The birthmark was to grow darker as the years passed, but now it was the same shade as her goldflecked eyes, which, to the end, were as steady and clean as rain.

Their friendship was as intense as it was sudden. They found relief in each other's personality. Although both were unshaped, formless things, Nel seemed stronger and more consistent than Sula, who could hardly be counted on to sustain any emotion for more than three minutes. Yet there was one time when that was not true, when she held on to a mood for weeks, but even that was in defense of Nel.

Four white boys in their early teens, sons of some newly arrived Irish people, occasionally entertained themselves in the afternoon by harassing black schoolchildren. With shoes that pinched and woolen knickers that made red rings on their calves, they had come to this valley with their parents believing as they did that it was a promised land — green and shimmering with welcome. What they found was a strange accent, a pervasive fear of their religion and firm resistance to their attempts to find work. With one exception the older residents of Medallion scorned them. The one exception was the black community. Although some of the Negroes had been in Medallion before the Civil War (the town didn't even have a name then), if they had any hatred for these newcomers it didn't matter because it didn't show. As a matter of fact, baiting them was the one activity that the white Protestant residents concurred in. In part their place in this world was secured only when they echoed the old residents' attitude toward blacks.

These particular boys caught Nel once, and pushed her from hand to hand until they grew tired of the frightened helpless face. Because of that incident, Nel's route home from school became elaborate. She, and then Sula, managed to duck them for weeks until a chilly day in November when Sula said, "Let's us go on home the shortest way."

Nel blinked, but acquiesced. They walked up the street until they got to the bend of Carpenter's Road where the boys lounged on a disused well. Spotting their prey, the boys sauntered forward as though there were nothing in the world on their minds but the gray sky. Hardly able to control their grins, they stood like a gate blocking the path. When the girls were three feet in front of the boys, Sula reached into her coat pocket and pulled out Eva's paring knife. The boys stopped short, exchanged looks and dropped all pretense of innocence. This was going to be better than they thought. They were going to try and fight back, and with a knife. Maybe they could get an arm around one of their waists, or tear . . .

Sula squatted down in the dirt road and put everything down on the ground: her lunchpail, her reader, her mittens, her slate. Holding the knife in her right hand, she pulled the slate toward her and pressed her left forefinger down hard on its edge. Her aim was determined but inaccurate.

She slashed off only the tip of her finger. The four boys stared open-mouthed at the wound and the scrap of flesh, like a button mushroom, curling in the cherry blood that ran into the corners of the slate.

Sula raised her eyes to them. Her voice was quiet. "If I can do that to myself, what you suppose I'll do to you?"

The shifting dirt was the only way Nel knew that they were moving away; she was looking at Sula's face, which seemed miles and miles away.

But toughness was not their quality — adventuresomeness was — and a mean determination to explore everything that interested them, from one-eyed chickens high-stepping in their penned yards to Mr. Buckland Reed's gold teeth, from the sound of sheets flapping in the wind to the labels on Tar Baby's wine bottles. And they had no priorities. They could be distracted from watching a fight with mean razors by the glorious smell of hot tar being poured by roadmen two hundred yards away.

In the safe harbor of each other's company they could afford to abandon the ways of other people and concentrate on their own perceptions of things. When Mrs. Wright reminded Nel to pull her nose, she would do it enthusiastically but without the least hope in the world.

"While you sittin' there, honey, go 'head and pull your nose."

"It hurts, Mamma."

"Don't you want a nice nose when you grow up?"

After she met Sula, Nel slid the clothespin under the blanket as soon as she got in the bed. And although there was still the hateful hot comb to suffer through each Saturday evening, its consequences — smooth hair — no longer interested her.

Joined in mutual admiration they watched each day as though it were a movie arranged for their amusement. The new theme they were now discovering was men. So they met regularly, without even planning it, to walk down the road to Edna Finch's Mellow House, even though it was too cool for ice cream.

Then summer came. A summer limp with the weight of blossomed things. Heavy sunflowers weeping over fences; iris curling and browning at the edges far away from their purple hearts; ears of corn letting their auburn hair wind down to their stalks. And the boys. The beautiful, beautiful boys who dotted the landscape like jewels, split the air with their shouts in the field, and thickened the river with their shining wet backs. Even their footsteps left a smell of smoke behind.

It was in that summer, the summer of their twelfth year, the summer of the beautiful black boys, that they became skittish, frightened and bold — all at the same time.

In that mercury mood in July, Sula and Nel wandered about the Bottom barefoot looking for mischief. They decided to go down by the river where the boys sometimes swam. Nel waited on the porch of 7 Carpenter's Road while Sula ran into the house to go to the toilet. On the way up the stairs, she passed the kitchen where Hannah sat with two friends, Patsy and Valentine. The two women were fanning themselves and watching Hannah put down some dough, all talking casually about one thing and another, and had gotten around, when Sula passed by, to the problems of child rearing.

"They a pain."

"Yeh. Wish I'd listened to mamma. She told me not to have 'em too soon."

"Any time atall is too soon for me."

"Oh, I don't know. My Rudy minds his daddy. He just wild with me. Be glad when he growed and gone."

Hannah smiled and said, "Shut your mouth. You love the ground he pee on."

"Sure I do. But he still a pain. Can't help loving your own child. No matter what they do."

"Well, Hester grown now and I can't say love is exactly what I feel."

"Sure you do. You love her, like I love Sula. I just don't like her. That's the difference."

"Guess so. Likin' them is another thing."

"Sure. They different people, you know . . ."

She only heard Hannah's words, and the pronouncement sent her flying up the stairs. In bewilderment, she stood at the window fingering the curtain edge, aware of a sting in her eye. Nel's call floated up and into the window, pulling her away from dark thoughts back into the bright, hot daylight.

They ran most of the way.

Heading toward the wide part of the river where trees grouped themselves in families darkening the earth below. They passed some boys swimming and clowning in the water, shrouding their words in laughter.

They ran in the sunlight, creating their

own breeze, which pressed their dresses into their damp skin. Reaching a kind of square of four leaf-locked trees which promised cooling, they flung themselves into the four-cornered shade to taste their lip sweat and contemplate the wildness that had come upon them so suddenly. They lay in the grass, their foreheads almost touching, their bodies stretched away from each other at a 180-degree angle. Sula's head rested on her arm, an undone braid coiled around her wrist. Nel leaned on her elbows and worried long blades of grass with her fingers. Underneath their dresses flesh tightened and shivered in the high coolness, their small breasts just now beginning to create some pleasant discomfort when they were lying on their stomachs.

Sula lifted her head and joined Nel in the grass play. In concert, without ever meeting each other's eyes, they stroked the blades up and down, up and down. Nel found a thick twig and, with her thumbnail, pulled away its bark until it was stripped to a smooth, creamy innocence. Sula looked about and found one too. When both twigs were undressed Nel moved easily to the next stage and began tearing up rooted grass to make a bare spot of earth. When a generous clearing was made, Sula traced intricate patterns in it with her twig. At first Nel was content to do the same. But soon she grew impatient and poked her twig rhythmically and intensely into the earth, making a small neat hole that grew deeper and wider with the least manipulation of her twig. Sula copied her, and soon each had a hole the size of a cup. Nel began a more strenuous digging and, rising to her knee, was careful to scoop out the dirt as she made her hole deeper. Together they worked until the two holes were one and the same. When the depression was the size of a small dishpan, Nel's twig broke. With a gesture of disgust she threw the pieces into the hole they had made. Sula threw hers in too. Nel saw a bottle cap and tossed it in as well. Each then looked around for more debris to throw into the hole: paper, bits of glass, butts of cigarettes, until all of the small defiling things they could find were collected there. Carefully they replaced the soil and covered the entire grave with uprooted grass.

Neither one had spoken a word.

They stood up, stretched, then gazed out over the swift dull water as an unspeakable restlessness and agitation held them. At the same instant each girl heard footsteps in the grass. A little boy in too big knickers was coming up from the lower bank of the river. He stopped when he saw them and picked his nose.

"Your mamma tole you to stop eatin' snot, Chicken," Nel hollered at him through cupped hands.

"Shut up," he said, still picking.

"Come up here and say that."

"Leave him 'lone, Nel. Come here, Chicken. Lemme show you something."

"Naw."

"You scared we gone take your bugger away?"

"Leave him 'lone, I said. Come on, Chicken. Look. I'll help you climb a tree."

Chicken looked at the tree Sula was pointing to — a big double beech with low branches and lots of bends for sitting.

He moved slowly toward her.

"Come on, Chicken, I'll help you up."

Still picking his nose, his eyes wide, he came to where they were standing. Sula took him by the hand and coaxed him along. When they reached the base of the beech, she lifted him to the first branch, saying, "Go on. Go on. I got you." She followed the boy, steadying him, when he needed it, with her hand and her reassuring voice. When they were as high as they could go, Sula pointed to the far side of the river.

"See? Bet you never saw that far before, did you?"

"Uh uh."

"Now look down there." They both leaned a little and peered through the leaves at Nel standing below, squinting up at them. From their height she looked small and foreshortened.

Chicken Little laughed.

"Y'all better come on down before you break your neck," Nel hollered.

"I ain't never coming down," the boy hollered back.

"Yeah. We better. Come on, Chicken."

"Naw. Lemme go."

"Yeah, Chicken. Come on, now."

Sula pulled his leg gently.

"Lemme go."

"OK, I'm leavin' you." She started on.

"Wait!" he screamed.

Sula stopped and together they slowly worked their way down.

Chicken was still elated. "I was way up there, wasn't I? Wasn't I? I'm a tell my brovver."

Sula and Nel began to mimic him: "I'm a tell my brovver; I'm a tell my brovver."

Sula picked him up by his hands and swung him outward then around and around. His knickers ballooned and his shrieks of frightened joy startled the birds and the fat grasshoppers. When he slipped from her hands and sailed away out over the water they could still hear his bubbly laughter.

The water darkened and closed quickly over the place where Chicken Little sank. The pressure of his hard and tight little fingers was still in Sula's palms as she stood looking at the closed place in the water. They expected him to come back up, laughing. Both girls stared at the water.

Nel spoke first. "Somebody saw." A figure appeared briefly on the opposite shore.

The only house over there was Shadrack's. Sula glanced at Nel. Terror widened her nostrils. Had he seen?

The water was so peaceful now. There was nothing but the baking sun and something newly missing. Sula cupped her face for an instant, then turned and ran up to the little plank bridge that crossed the river to Shadrack's house. There was no path. It was as though neither Shadrack nor anyone else ever came this way.

Her running was swift and determined,

but when she was close to the three little steps that led to his porch, fear crawled into her stomach and only the something newly missing back there in the river made it possible for her to walk up the three steps and knock at the door.

No one answered. She started back, but thought again of the peace of the river. Shadrack would be inside, just behind the door ready to pounce on her. Still she could not go back. Ever so gently she pushed the door with the tips of her fingers and heard only the hinges weep. More. And then she was inside. Alone. The neatness, the order startled her, but more surprising was the restfulness. Everything was so tiny, so common, so unthreatening. Perhaps this was not the house of the Shad. The terrible Shad who walked about with his penis out, who peed in front of ladies and girl-children, the only black who could curse white people and get away with it, who drank in the road from the mouth of the bottle, who shouted and shook in the streets. This cottage? This sweet old cottage? With its made-up bed? With its rag rug and wooden table? Sula stood in the middle of the little room and in her wonder forgot what she had come for until a sound at the door made her jump. He was there in the doorway looking at her. She had not heard his coming and now he was looking at her.

More in embarrassment than terror she averted her glance. When she called up enough courage to look back at him, she saw his hand resting upon the door frame. His fingers, barely touching the wood, were arranged in a graceful arc. Relieved and encouraged (no one with hands like that, no one with fingers that curved around wood so tenderly could kill her), she walked past him out of the door, feeling his gaze turning, turning with her.

At the edge of the porch, gathering the wisps of courage that were fast leaving her, she turned once more to look at him, to ask him . . . had he . . . ?

He was smiling, a great smile, heavy with lust and time to come. He nodded his head as though answering a question, and said, in a pleasant conversational tone, a tone of cooled butter, "Always."

Sula fled down the steps, and shot through the greenness and the baking sun back to Nel and the dark closed place in the water. There she collapsed in tears.

Nel quieted her. "Sh, sh. Don't, don't. You didn't mean it. It ain't your fault. Sh. Sh. Come on, le's go, Sula. Come on, now.

Was he there? Did he see? Where's the belt to your dress?"

Sula shook her head while she searched her waist for the belt.

Finally she stood up and allowed Nel to lead her away. "He said, 'Always. Always.'"

"What?"

Sula covered her mouth as they walked down the hill. Always. He had answered a question she had not asked, and its promise licked at her feet.

A bargeman, poling away from the shore, found Chicken late that afternoon stuck in some rocks and weeds, his knickers ballooning about his legs. He would have left him there but noticed that it was a child, not an old black man, as it first appeared, and he prodded the body loose, netted it and hauled it aboard. He shook his head in disgust at the kind of parents who would drown their own children. When, he wondered, will those people ever be anything but animals, fit for nothing but substitutes for mules, only mules didn't kill each other the way niggers did. He dumped Chicken Little into a burlap sack and tossed him next to some egg crates and boxes of wool cloth. Later, sitting down to smoke on an empty lard tin, still bemused by God's curse and the terrible burden his own kind had of elevating Ham's sons, he suddenly became alarmed by the thought that the corpse in this heat would have a terrible odor, which might get into the fabric of his woolen cloth. He dragged the sack away and hooked it over the side, so that the Chicken's body was half in and half out of the water.

Wiping the sweat from his neck, he reported his find to the sheriff at Porter's Landing, who said they didn't have no niggers in their county, but that some lived in those hills 'cross the river, up above Medallion. The bargeman said he couldn't go all the way back there, it was every bit of two miles. The sheriff said whyn't he throw it on back into the water. The bargeman said he never shoulda taken it out in the first place. Finally they got the man who ran the ferry twice a day to agree to take it over in the morning.

That was why Chicken Little was missing for three days and didn't get to the embalmer's until the fourth day, by which time he was unrecognizable to almost everybody who once knew him, and even his mother wasn't deep down sure, except that it just had to be him since nobody could find him. When she saw his clothes lying on the table in the basement of the mortuary, her mouth snapped shut, and when she saw his body her mouth flew wide open again and it was seven hours before she was able to close it and make the first sound.

So the coffin was closed.

The Junior Choir, dressed in white, sang "Nearer My God to Thee" and "Precious Memories," their eyes fastened on the songbooks they did not need, for this was the first time their voices had presided at a real-life event.

Nel and Sula did not touch hands or look at each other during the funeral. There was a space, a separateness, between them. Nel's legs had turned to granite and she expected the sheriff or Reverend Deal's pointing finger at any moment. Although she knew she had "done nothing," she felt convicted and hanged right there in the pew — two rows down from her parents in the children's section.

Sula simply cried. Soundlessly and with no heaving and gasping for breath, she let the tears roll into her mouth and slide down her chin to dot the front of her dress.

As Reverend Deal moved into his sermon, the hands of the women unfolded like pairs of raven's wings and flew high above their hats in the air. They did not hear all of what he said; they heard the one word, or phrase, or inflection that was for them the connection between the event and themselves. For some it was the term "Sweet Jesus." And they saw the Lamb's eye and the truly innocent victim: themselves. They acknowledged the innocent child hiding in the corner of their hearts, holding a sugar-and-butter sandwich. That one. The one who lodged deep in their fat, thin, old, young skin, and was the one the world had hurt. Or they thought of their son newly killed and remembered his legs in short pants and wondered where the bullet went in. Or they remembered how dirty the room looked when their father left home and wondered if that is the way the slim, young Jew felt, he who for them was both son and lover and in whose downy face they could see the sugar-and-butter sandwiches and feel the oldest and most devastating pain there is: not the pain of childhood, but the remembrance of it.

Then they left their pews. For with some emotions one has to stand. They spoke, for they were full and needed to say. They swayed, for the rivulets of grief or of ecstasy must be rocked. And when they thought of all that life and death locked into that little closed coffin they danced and screamed, not to protest God's will but to acknowledge it and confirm once more their conviction that the only way to avoid the Hand of God is to get in it.

In the colored part of the cemetery, they sank Chicken Little in between his grandfather and an aunt. Butterflies flew in and out of the bunches of field flowers now loosened from the top of the bier and lying in a small heap at the edge of the grave. The heat had gone, but there was still no breeze to lift the hair of the willows.

Nel and Sula stood some distance away from the grave, the space that had sat between them in the pews had dissolved. They held hands and knew that only the coffin would lie in the earth; the bubbly laughter and the press of fingers in the palm would stay aboveground forever. At first, as they stood there, their hands were clenched together. They relaxed slowly until during the walk back home their fingers were laced in as gentle a clasp as that of any two young girlfriends trotting up the road on a summer day wondering what happened to butterflies in the winter.

1923

The second strange thing was Hannah's coming into her mother's room with an empty bowl and a peck of Kentucky Wonders and saying, "Mamma, did you ever love us?" She sang the words like a small child saying a piece at Easter, then knelt to spread a newspaper on the floor and set the basket on it; the bowl she tucked in the space between her legs. Eva, who was just sitting there fanning herself with the cardboard fan from Mr. Hodges' funeral parlor, listened to the silence that followed Hannah's words, then said, "Scat!" to the deweys who were playing chain gang near the window. With the shoelaces of each of them tied to the laces of the others, they stumbled and tumbled out of Eva's room.

"Now," Eva looked up across from her wagon at her daughter. "Give me that again. Flat out to fit my head."

"I mean, did you? You know. When we was little."

Eva's hand moved snail-like down her thigh toward her stump, but stopped short of it to realign a pleat. "No. I don't reckon I did. Not the way you thinkin'."

"Oh, well. I was just wonderin'." Hannah appeared to be through with the subject.

"An evil wonderin' if I ever heard one." Eva was not through.

"I didn't mean nothing by it, Mamma."

"What you mean you didn't *mean* nothing by it? How you gone not mean something by it?"

Hannah pinched the tips off the Kentucky Wonders and snapped their long pods. What with the sound of the cracking and snapping and her swift-fingered movements, she seemed to be playing a complicated instrument. Eva watched her a moment and then said, "You gone can them?"

"No. They for tonight."

"Thought you was gone can some."

"Uncle Paul ain't brought me none yet. A peck ain't enough to can. He say he got two bushels for me."

"Triflin'."

"Oh, he all right."

"Sho he all right. Everybody all right. 'Cept Mamma. Mamma the only one ain't

97

all right. Cause she didn't *love* us."

"Awww, Mamma."

"Awww, Mamma? Awww, Mamma? You settin' here with your healthy-ass self and ax me did I love you? Them big old eyes in your head would a been two holes full of maggots if I hadn't."

"I didn't mean that, Mamma. I know you fed us and all. I was talkin' 'bout something else. Like. Like. Playin' with us. Did you ever, you know, play with us?"

"Play? Wasn't nobody playin' in 1895. Just 'cause you got it good now you think it was always this good? 1895 was a killer, girl. Things was bad. Niggers was dying like flies. Stepping tall, ain't you? Uncle Paul gone bring me *two* bushels. Yeh. And they's a melon downstairs, ain't they? And I bake every Saturday, and Shad brings fish on Friday, and they's a pork barrel full of meal, and we float eggs in a crock of vinegar . . ."

"Mamma, what you talkin' 'bout?"

"I'm talkin' 'bout 18 and 95 when I set in that house five days with you and Pearl and Plum and three beets, you snake-eyed ungrateful hussy. What would I look like leapin' 'round that little old room playin' with youngins with three beets to my name?"

"I know 'bout them beets, Mamma. You told us that a million times."

"Yeah? Well? Don't that count? Ain't that love? You want me to tinkle you under the jaw and forget 'bout them sores in your mouth? Pearl was shittin' worms and I was supposed to play rang-around-the-rosie?"

"But Mamma, they had to be some time when you wasn't thinkin' 'bout . . ."

"No time. They wasn't no time. Not none. Soon as I got one day done here come a night. With you all coughin' and me watchin' so TB wouldn't take you off and if you was sleepin' quiet I thought, O Lord, they dead and put my hand over your mouth to feel if the breath was comin' what you talkin' 'bout did I love you girl I stayed alive for you can't you get that through your thick head or what is that between your ears, heifer?"

Hannah had enough beans now. With some tomatoes and hot bread, she thought, that would be enough for everybody, especially since the deweys didn't eat vegetables no how and Eva never made them and Tar Baby was living off air and music these days. She picked up the basket and stood with it and the bowl of beans over her mother. Eva's face was still asking her last question. Hannah looked into her mother's eyes.

"But what about Plum? What'd you kill Plum for, Mamma?"

It was a Wednesday in August and the ice wagon was coming and coming. You could hear bits of the driver's song. Now Mrs. Jackson would be tipping down her porch steps. "Jes a piece. You got a lil ole piece layin' 'round in there you could spare?" And as he had since the time of the pigeons, the iceman would hand her a lump of ice saying, "Watch it now, Mrs. Jackson. That straw'll tickle your pretty neck to death."

Eva listened to the wagon coming and thought about what it must be like in the icehouse. She leaned back a little and closed her eyes trying to see the insides of the icehouse. It was a dark, lovely picture in this heat, until it reminded her of that winter night in the outhouse holding her baby in the dark, her fingers searching for his asshole and the last bit of lard scooped from the sides of the can, held deliberately on the tip of her middle finger, the last bit of lard to keep from hurting him when she slid her finger in and all because she had broken the slop jar and the rags had frozen. The last food staple in the house she had rammed up her baby's behind to keep from hurting him too much when she opened up his bowels to pull the stools out. He had been screaming fit to kill, but when she found his hole at last and stuck her finger up in it, the shock was so great he was suddenly quiet. Even now on the hottest day anyone in Medallion could remember — a day so hot flies slept and cats were splaying their fur like quills, a day so hot pregnant wives leaned up against trees and cried, and women remembering some three-month-old hurt put ground glass in their lovers' food and the men looked at the food and wondered if there was glass in it and ate it anyway because it was too hot to resist eating it — even on this hottest of days in the hot spell, Eva shivered from the biting cold and stench of that outhouse.

Hannah was waiting. Watching her mother's eyelids. When Eva spoke at last it was with two voices. Like two people were talking at the same time, saying the same thing, one a fraction of a second behind the other.

"He give me such a time. Such a time. Look like he didn't even want to be born. But he come on out. Boys is hard to bear. You wouldn't know that but they is. It was such a carryin' on to get him born and to keep him alive. Just to keep his little heart beating and his little old lungs cleared and look like when he came back from that war he wanted to git back in. After all that carryin' on, just gettin' him out and keepin' him alive, he wanted to crawl back in my womb and well . . . I ain't got the room no more even if he could do it. There wasn't space for him in my womb. And he was crawlin' back. Being helpless and thinking baby thoughts and dreaming baby dreams and messing up his pants again and smiling all the time. I had room enough in my heart, but not in my womb, not no more. I birthed him once. I couldn't do it again. He was growed, a big old thing. Godhavemercy, I couldn't birth him twice. I'd be laying here at night and he be downstairs in that room, but when I closed my eyes I'd see him . . . six feet tall smilin' and crawlin' up the stairs quietlike so I wouldn't hear and opening the door soft so I wouldn't hear and he'd be creepin' to the bed trying to spread my legs trying to get back up in my womb. He was a man, girl, a big old growed-up man. I didn't have that much room. I kept on dreaming it. Dreaming it and I knowed it was true. One night it wouldn't be no dream. It'd be true and I would have done it, would have let him if I'd've had the room but a big man can't be a baby all

102

wrapped up inside his mamma no more; he suffocate. I done everything I could to make him leave me and go on and live and be a man but he wouldn't and I had to keep him out so I just thought of a way he could die like a man not all scrunched up inside my womb, but like a man."

Eva couldn't see Hannah clearly for the tears, but she looked up at her anyway and said, by way of apology or explanation or perhaps just by way of neatness, "But I held him close first. Real close. Sweet Plum. My baby boy."

Long after Hannah turned and walked out of the room, Eva continued to call his name while her fingers lined up the pleats in her dress.

Hannah went off to the kitchen, her old man's slippers plopping down the stairs and over the hardwood floors. She turned the spigot on, letting water break up the tight knots of Kentucky Wonders and float them to the top of the bowl. She swirled them about with her fingers, poured the water off and repeated the process. Each time the green tubes rose to the surface she felt elated and collected whole hand-fuls at a time to drop in twos and threes back into the water.

Through the window over the sink she

could see the deweys still playing chain gang; their ankles bound one to the other, they tumbled, struggled back to their feet and tried to walk single file. Hens strutted by with one suspicious eye on the deweys, another on the brick fireplace where sheets and mason jars were boiled. Only the deweys could play in this heat. Hannah put the Kentucky Wonders over the fire and, struck by a sudden sleepiness, she went off to lie down in the front room. It was even hotter there, for the windows were shut to keep out the sunlight. Hannah straightened the shawl that draped the couch and lay down. She dreamed of a wedding in a red bridal gown until Sula came in and woke her.

But before the second strange thing, there had been the wind, which was the first. The very night before the day Hannah had asked Eva if she had ever loved them, the wind tore over the hills rattling roofs and loosening doors. Everything shook, and although the people were frightened they thought it meant rain and welcomed it. Windows fell out and trees lost arms. People waited up half the night for the first crack of lightning. Some had even uncovered barrels to catch the rain water, which they loved to drink and cook in. They waited in vain, for no lightning no thunder no rain came. The wind just swept through, took what dampness there was out of the air, messed up the yards, and went on. The hills of the Bottom, as always, protected the valley part of town where the white people lived, and the next morning all the people were grateful because there was a dryer heat. So they set about their work early, for it was canning time, and who knew but what the wind would come back this time with a cooling rain. The men who worked in the valley got up at four thirty in the morning and looked at the sky where the sun was already rising like a hot white bitch. They beat the brims of their hats against their legs before putting them on and trudged down the road like old promises nobody wanted kept.

On Thursday, when Hannah brought Eva her fried tomatoes and soft scrambled eggs with the white left out for good luck, she mentioned her dream of the wedding in the red dress. Neither one bothered to look it up for they both knew the number was 522. Eva said she'd play it when Mr. Buckland Reed came by. Later she would remember it as the third strange thing. She had thought it odd even then, but the red in the dream confused her. But she wasn't certain that it was third or not because Sula was acting up, fretting the deweys and meddling the newly married couple. Because she was thirteen, everybody supposed her nature was coming down, but it was hard to put up with her sulking and irritation. The birthmark over her eye was getting darker and looked more and more like a stem and rose. She was dropping things and eating food that belonged to the newly married couple and started in to worrying everybody that the deweys needed a bath and she was going to give it to them. The deweys, who went wild at the thought of water, were crying and thundering all over the house like colts.

"We ain't got to, do we? Do we got to do what she says? It ain't Saturday." They even woke up Tar Baby, who came out of his room to look at them and then left the house in search of music.

Hannah ignored them and kept on bringing mason jars out of the cellar and washing them. Eva banged on the floor with her stick but nobody came. By noon it was quiet. The deweys had escaped, Sula was either in her room or gone off somewhere. The newly married couple, energized by their morning lovemaking, had gone to look for a day's work happily certain that they would find none.

The air all over the Bottom got heavy with peeled fruit and boiling vegetables. Fresh corn, tomatoes, string beans, melon rinds. The women, the children and the old men who had no jobs were putting up for a winter they understood so well. Peaches were stuffed into jars and black cherries (later, when it got cooler, they would put up jellies and preserves). The greedy canned as many as forty-two a day even though some of them, like Mrs. Jackson, who ate ice, had jars from 1920.

Before she trundled her wagon over to the dresser to get her comb, Eva looked out the window and saw Hannah bending to light the yard fire. And that was the fifth (or fourth, if you didn't count Sula's craziness) strange thing. She couldn't find her comb. Nobody moved stuff in Eva's room except to clean and then they put everything right back. But Eva couldn't find it anywhere. One hand pulling her braids loose, the other searching the dresser drawers, she had just begun to get irritated when she felt it in her blouse drawer. Then she trundled back to the window to catch a breeze, if one took a mind to come by, while she combed her hair. She rolled up to the window and it was then she saw Hannah burning. The flames from the yard fire were licking the blue cotton dress, making her dance. Eva knew there was time for nothing in this world other than the time it took to get there and cover her daughter's body with her own. She lifted her heavy frame up on her good leg, and with fists and arms smashed the window-pane. Using her stump as a support on the window sill, her good leg as a lever, she threw herself out of the window. Cut and bleeding she clawed the air trying to aim her body toward the flaming, dancing figure. She missed and came crashing down some twelve feet from Hannah's smoke. Stunned but still conscious, Eva dragged herself toward her firstborn, but Hannah, her senses lost, went flying out of the yard gesturing and bobbing like a sprung jack-in-the-box.

Mr. and Mrs. Suggs, who had set up their canning apparatus in their front yard, saw her running, dancing toward them. They whispered, "Jesus, Jesus," and to-gether hoisted up their tub of water in which tight red tomatoes floated and threw it on the smoke-and-flame-bound woman. The water did put out the flames, but it also made steam, which seared to sealing all that was left of the beautiful Hannah Peace. She lay there on the wooden sidewalk planks, twitching lightly among the smashed tomatoes, her face a mask of agony so intense that for years the people who gathered 'round would shake their heads at the recollection of it.

Somebody covered her legs with a shirt. A woman unwrapped her head rag and placed it on Hannah's shoulder. Somebody else ran to Dick's Fresh Food and Sundries to call the ambulance. The rest stood there as helpless as sunflowers leaning on a fence. The deweys came and stepped in the tomatoes, their eyes raked with wonder. Two cats sidled through the legs of the crowd, sniffing the burned flesh. The vomiting of a young girl finally broke the profound silence and caused the women to talk to each other and to God. In the midst of calling Jesus they heard the hollow clang of the ambulance bell struggling up the hill, but not the "Help me, ya'll" that the dying woman whispered. Then somebody remembered to go and see about Eva. They found her on her stomach by the forsythia bushes calling Hannah's name and dragging her body through the sweet peas and clover that grew under the forsythia by the side of the house. Mother and daughter were placed on stretchers and carried to the ambulance. Eva was wide awake. The blood from her face cuts filled her eyes so she could not see, could only smell the familiar odor of cooked flesh.

Hannah died on the way to the hospital. Or so they said. In any case, she had already begun to bubble and blister so badly that the coffin had to be kept closed at the funeral and the women who washed the body and dressed it for death wept for her burned hair and wrinkled breasts as though they themselves had been her lovers.

When Eva got to the hospital they put her stretcher on the floor, so preoccupied with the hot and bubbling flesh of the other (some of them had never seen so extreme a burn case before) they forgot Eva, who would have bled to death except Old Willy Fields, the orderly, saw blood staining his just-mopped floors and went to find out where it was coming from. Recognizing Eva at once he shouted to a nurse, who came to see if the bloody one-legged black woman was alive or dead. From then on Willy boasted that he had saved Eva's life — an indisputable fact which she herself admitted and for which she cursed him every day for thirty-seven years thereafter and would have cursed him for the rest of her life except by then she was already ninety years old and forgot things.

Lying in the colored ward of the hospital, which was a screened corner of a larger ward, Eva mused over the perfection of the judgment against her. She remembered the wedding dream and recalled that weddings always meant death. And the red gown, well that was the fire, as she should have known. She remembered something else too, and try as she might to deny it, she knew that as she lay on the ground trying to drag herself through the sweet peas and clover to get to Hannah, she had seen Sula standing on the back porch just looking. When Eva, who was never one to hide the faults of her children, mentioned what she thought she'd seen to a few friends, they said it was natural. Sula was probably struck dumb, as anybody would be who saw her own mamma burn up. Eva said yes, but inside she disagreed and remained convinced that Sula had watched Hannah burn not because she was paralyzed, but because she was interested.

1927

Old people were dancing with little children. Young boys with their sisters, and the church women who frowned on any bodily expression of joy (except when the hand of God commanded it) tapped their feet. Somebody (the groom's father, everybody said) had poured a whole pint jar of cane liquor into the punch, so even the men who did not sneak out the back door to have a shot, as well as the women who let nothing stronger than Black Draught enter their blood, were tipsy. A small boy stood at the Victrola turning its handle and smiling at the sound of Bert Williams' "Save a Little Dram for Me."

Even Helene Wright had mellowed with the cane, waving away apologies for drinks spilled on her rug and paying no attention whatever to the chocolate cake lying on the arm of her red-velvet sofa. The tea roses above her left breast had slipped from the brooch that fastened them and were hanging heads down. When her husband called her attention to the children wrapping themselves into her curtains, she merely smiled and said, "Oh, let them be." She was not only a little drunk, she was weary and had been for weeks. Her only child's wedding — the culmination of all she had been, thought or done in this world — had dragged from her energy and stamina even she did not know she possessed. Her house had to be thoroughly cleaned, chickens had to be plucked, cakes and pies made, and for weeks she, her friends and her daughter had been sewing. Now it was all happening and it took only a little cane juice to snap the cords of fatigue and damn the white curtains that she had pinned on the stretcher only the morning before. Once this day was over she would have a lifetime to rattle around in that house and repair the damage.

A real wedding, in a church, with a real reception afterward, was rare among the people of the Bottom. Expensive for one thing, and most newlyweds just went to the courthouse if they were not particular, or had the preacher come in and say a few words if they were. The rest just "took up" with one another. No invitations were sent.

There was no need for that formality. Folks just came, bringing a gift if they had one, none if they didn't. Except for those who worked in valley houses, most of them had never been to a big wedding; they simply assumed it was rather like a funeral except afterward you didn't have to walk all the way out to Beechnut Cemetery.

This wedding offered a special attraction, for the bridegroom was a handsome, well-liked man — the tenor of Mount Zion's Men's Quartet, who had an enviable reputation among the girls and a comfortable one among men. His name was Jude Greene, and with the pick of some eight or ten girls who came regularly to services to hear him sing, he had chosen Nel Wright.

He wasn't really aiming to get married. He was twenty then, and although his job as a waiter at the Hotel Medallion was a blessing to his parents and their seven other children, it wasn't nearly enough to support a wife. He had brought the subject up first on the day the word got out that the town was building a new road, tarmac, that would wind through Medallion on down to the river, where a great new bridge was to be built to connect Medallion to Porter's Landing, the town on the other side. The war over, a fake prosperity was still around. In a state of euphoria, with a hunger for more and more, the council of founders cast its eye toward a future that would certainly include trade from cross-river towns. Towns that needed more than a house raft to get to the merchants of Medallion. Work had already begun on the New River Road (the city had always meant to name it something else, something wonderful, but ten years later when the bridge idea was dropped for a tunnel it was still called the New River Road).

Along with a few other young black men, Jude had gone down to the shack where they were hiring. Three old colored men had already been hired, but not for the road work, just to do the picking up, food bringing and other small errands. These old men were close to feeble, not good for much else, and everybody was pleased they were taken on; still it was a shame to see those white men laughing with the grandfathers but shying away from the young black men who could tear that road up. The men like Jude who could do real work. Jude himself longed more than anybody else to be taken. Not just for the good money, more for the work itself. He wanted to swing the pick or kneel down with the string or shovel the gravel. His arms ached for something heavier than trays, for something dirtier than peelings; his feet wanted the heavy work shoes, not the thin-soled black shoes that the hotel required. More than anything he wanted the camaraderie of the road men: the lunch buckets, the hollering, the body movement that in the end produced something real, something he could point to. "I built that road," he could say. How much better sundown would be than the end of a day in the restaurant, where a good day's work was marked by the number of dirty plates and the weight of the garbage bin. "I built that road." People would walk over his sweat for years. Perhaps a sledge hammer would come crashing down on his foot, and when people asked him how come he limped, he could say, "Got that building the New Road."

It was while he was full of such dreams, his body already feeling the rough work clothes, his hands already curved to the pick handle, that he spoke to Nel about getting married. She seemed receptive but hardly anxious. It was after he stood in lines for six days running and saw the gang boss pick out thin-armed white boys from the Virginia hills and the bull-necked

Greeks and Italians and heard over and over, "Nothing else today. Come back tomorrow," that he got the message. So it was rage, rage and a determination to take on a man's role anyhow that made him press Nel about settling down. He needed some of his appetites filled, some posture of adulthood recognized, but mostly he wanted someone to care about his hurt, to care very deeply. Deep enough to hold him, deep enough to rock him, deep enough to ask, "How you feel? You all right? Want some coffee?" And if he were to be a man, that someone could no longer be his mother. He chose the girl who had always been kind, who had never seemed hell-bent to marry, who made the whole venture seem like his idea, his conquest.

The more he thought about marriage, the more attractive it became. Whatever his fortune, whatever the cut of his garment, there would always be the hem — the tuck and fold that hid his raveling edges; a someone sweet, industrious and loyal to shore him up. And in return he would shelter her, love her, grow old with her. Without that someone he was a waiter hanging around a kitchen like a woman. With her he was head of a household pinned to an unsatisfactory job out of necessity. The two of them together would make one Jude.

His fears lest his burst dream of road building discourage her were never realized. Nel's indifference to his hints about marriage disappeared altogether when she discovered his pain. Jude could see himself taking shape in her eyes. She actually wanted to help, to soothe, and was it true what Ajax said in the Time and a Half Pool Hall? That "all they want, man, is they own misery. Ax em to die for you and they yours for life."

Whether he was accurate in general, Ajax was right about Nel. Except for an occasional leadership role with Sula, she had no aggression. Her parents had succeeded in rubbing down to a dull glow any sparkle or splutter she had. Only with Sula did that quality have free reign, but their friendship was so close, they themselves had difficulty distinguishing one's thoughts from the other's. During all of her girlhood the only respite Nel had had from her stern and undemonstrative parents was Sula. When Jude began to hover around, she was flattered — all the girls liked him — and Sula made the enjoyment of his attentions keener simply because she seemed always to want Nel to shine. They never quarreled, those two, the way some girl-friends did over boys, or competed against each other for them. In those days a compliment to one was a compliment to the other, and cruelty to one was a challenge to the other.

Nel's response to Jude's shame and anger selected her away from Sula. And greater than her friendship was this new feeling of being needed by someone who saw her singly. She didn't even know she had a neck until Jude remarked on it, or that her smile was anything but the spreading of her lips until he saw it as a small miracle.

Sula was no less excited about the wedding. She thought it was the perfect thing to do following their graduation from general school. She wanted to be the bridesmaid. No others. And she encouraged Mrs. Wright to go all out, even to borrowing Eva's punch bowl. In fact, she handled most of the details very efficiently, capitalizing on the fact that most people were anxious to please her since she had lost her mamma only a few years back and they still remembered the agony in Hannah's face and the blood on Eva's.

So they danced up in the Bottom on the

second Saturday in June, danced at the wedding where everybody realized for the first time that except for their magnificent teeth, the deweys would never grow. They had been forty-eight inches tall for years now, and while their size was unusual it was not unheard of. The realization was based on the fact that they remained boys in mind. Mischievous, cunning, private and completely unhousebroken, their games and interests had not changed since Hannah had them all put into the first grade together.

Nel and Jude, who had been the stars all during the wedding, were forgotten finally as the reception melted into a dance, a feed, a gossip session, a playground and a love nest. For the first time that day they relaxed and looked at each other, and liked what they saw. They began to dance, pressed in among the others, and each one turned his thoughts to the night that was coming on fast. They had taken a house-keeping room with one of Jude's aunts (over the protest of Mrs. Wright, who had rooms to spare, but Nel didn't want to make love to her husband in her mother's house) and were getting restless to go there.

As if reading her thoughts, Jude leaned

down and whispered, "Me too." Nel smiled and rested her cheek on his shoulder. The veil she wore was too heavy to allow her to feel the core of the kiss he pressed on her head. When she raised her eyes to him for one more look of reassurance, she saw through the open door a slim figure in blue, gliding, with just a hint of a strut, down the path toward the road. One hand was pressed to the head to hold down the large hat against the warm June breeze. Even from the rear Nel could tell that it was Sula and that she was smiling; that something deep down in that litheness was amused. It would be ten years before they saw each other again, and their meeting would be thick with birds.

PART
TWO

1937

Accompanied by a plague of robins, Sula came back to Medallion. The little yam-breasted shuddering birds were everywhere, exciting very small children away from their usual welcome into a vicious stoning. Nobody knew why or from where they had come. What they did know was that you couldn't go anywhere without stepping in their pearly shit, and it was hard to hang up clothes, pull weeds or just sit on the front porch when robins were flying and dying all around you.

Although most of the people remembered the time when the sky was black for two hours with clouds and clouds of pigeons, and although they were accustomed to excesses in nature — too much heat, too much cold, too little rain, rain to flooding — they still dreaded the way a relatively trivial phenomenon could become sovereign in their lives and bend their minds to its will.

In spite of their fear, they reacted to an oppressive oddity, or what they called evil days, with an acceptance that bordered on welcome. Such evil must be avoided, they felt, and precautions must naturally be taken to protect themselves from it. But they let it run its course, fulfill itself, and never invented ways either to alter it, to annihilate it or to prevent its happening again. So also were they with people.

What was taken by outsiders to be slackness, slovenliness or even generosity was in fact a full recognition of the legitimacy of forces other than good ones. They did not believe doctors could heal — for them, none ever had done so. They did not believe death was accidental — life might be, but death was deliberate. They did not believe Nature was ever askew — only inconvenient. Plague and drought were as "natural" as springtime. If milk could curdle, God knows robins could fall. The purpose of evil was to survive it and they determined (without ever knowing they had made up their minds to do it) to survive floods, white people, tuberculosis, famine and ignorance. They knew anger well but not despair, and they didn't stone sinners for the same reason they didn't commit suicide — it was beneath them.

Sula stepped off the Cincinnati Flyer into the robin shit and began the long climb up into the Bottom. She was dressed in a manner that was as close to a movie star as anyone would ever see. A black crepe dress splashed with pink and yellow zinnias, foxtails, a black felt hat with the veil of net lowered over one eye. In her right hand was a black purse with a beaded clasp and in her left a red leather traveling case, so small, so charming — no one had seen anything like it ever before, including the mayor's wife and the music teacher, both of whom had been to Rome.

Walking up the hill toward Carpenter's Road, the heels and sides of her pumps edged with drying bird shit, she attracted the glances of old men sitting on stone benches in front of the courthouse, housewives throwing buckets of water on their sidewalks, and high school students on their way home for lunch. By the time she reached the Bottom, the news of her return had brought the black people out on their porches or to their windows. There were scattered hellos and nods but mostly stares. A little boy ran up to her saying, "Carry yo' bag, ma'am?" Before Sula could answer his mother had called him, "You, John. Get back in here."

At Eva's house there were four dead robins on the walk. Sula stopped and with her toe pushed them into the bordering grass.

Eva looked at Sula pretty much the same way she had looked at BoyBoy that time when he returned after he'd left her without a dime or a prospect of one. She was sitting in her wagon, her back to the window she had jumped out of (now all boarded up) setting fire to the hair she had combed out of her head. When Sula opened the door she raised her eyes and said, "I might have knowed them birds meant something. Where's your coat?"

Sula threw herself on Eva's bed. "The rest of my stuff will be on later."

"I should hope so. Them little old furry tails ain't going to do you no more good than they did the fox that was wearing them."

"Don't you say hello to nobody when you ain't seen them for ten years?"

"If folks let somebody know where they is and when they coming, then other folks can get ready for them. If they don't — if they just pop in all sudden like — then they got to take whatever mood they find."

"How you been doing, Big Mamma?"

"Gettin' by. Sweet of you to ask. You was quick enough when you wanted something. When you needed a little change or . . ."

"Don't talk to me about how much you gave me, Big Mamma, and how much I owe you or none of that."

"Oh? I ain't supposed to mention it?"

"OK. Mention it." Sula shrugged and turned over on her stomach, her buttocks toward Eva.

"You ain't been in this house ten seconds and already you starting something."

"Takes two, Big Mamma."

"Well, don't let your mouth start nothing that your ass can't stand. When you gone to get married? You need to have some babies. It'll settle you."

"I don't want to make somebody else. I want to make myself."

"Selfish. Ain't no woman got no business floatin' around without no man."

"You did."

"Not by choice."

"Mamma did."

"Not by choice, I said. It ain't right for you to want to stay off by yourself. You need . . . I'm a tell you what you need."

Sula sat up. "I need you to shut your mouth."

"Don't nobody talk to me like that. Don't nobody . . ."

"This body does. Just 'cause you was bad enough to cut off your own leg you think you got a right to kick everybody with the stump."

"Who said I cut off my leg?"

"Well, you stuck it under a train to collect insurance."

"Hold on, you lyin' heifer!"

"I aim to."

"Bible say honor thy father and thy mother that thy days may be long upon the land thy God giveth thee."

"Mamma must have skipped that part. Her days wasn't too long."

"Pus mouth! God's going to strike you!"

"Which God? The one watched you burn Plum?"

"Don't talk to me about no burning. You watched your own mamma. You crazy roach! You the one should have been burnt!"

"But I ain't. Got that? I ain't. Any more fires in this house, I'm lighting them!"

"Hellfire don't need lighting and it's already burning in you . . ."

"Whatever's burning in me is mine!"

"Amen!"

"And I'll split this town in two and everything in it before I'll let you put it out!"

"Pride goeth before a fall."

"What the hell do I care about falling?"

"Amazing Grace."

"You sold your life for twenty-three dollars a month."

"You throwed yours away."

"It's mine to throw."

"One day you gone need it."

"But not you. I ain't never going to need you. And you know what? Maybe one night when you dozing in that wagon flicking flies and swallowing spit, maybe I'll just tip on up here with some kerosene and — who knows — you may make the brightest flame of them all."

So Eva locked her door from then on. But it did no good. In April two men came with a stretcher and she didn't even have time to comb her hair before they strapped her to a piece of canvas.

When Mr. Buckland Reed came by to pick up the number, his mouth sagged at the sight of Eva being carried out and Sula holding some papers against the wall, at the bottom of which, just above the word "guardian," she very carefully wrote Miss Sula Mae Peace.

⬡⬡⬡

Nel alone noticed the peculiar quality of

131

the May that followed the leaving of the birds. It had a sheen, a glimmering as of green, rain-soaked Saturday nights (lit by the excitement of newly installed street lights); of lemon-yellow afternoons bright with iced drinks and splashes of daffodils. It showed in the damp faces of her children and the river-smoothness of their voices. Even her own body was not immune to the magic. She would sit on the floor to sew as she had done as a girl, fold her legs up under her or do a little dance that fitted some tune in her head. There were easy sun-washed days and purple dusks in which Tar Baby sang "Abide With Me" at prayer meetings, his lashes darkened by tears, his silhouette limp with regret against the whitewashed walls of Greater Saint Matthew's. Nel listened and was moved to smile. To smile at the sheer loveliness that pressed in from the windows and touched his grief, making it a pleasure to behold.

Although it was she alone who saw this magic, she did not wonder at it. She knew it was all due to Sula's return to the Bottom. It was like getting the use of an eye back, having a cataract removed. Her old friend had come home. Sula. Who made her laugh, who made her see old things with new eyes, in whose presence she felt clever, gentle and a little raunchy. Sula, whose past she had lived through and with whom the present was a constant sharing of perceptions. Talking to Sula had always been a conversation with herself. Was there anyone else before whom she could never be foolish? In whose view inadequacy was mere idiosyncrasy, a character trait rather than a deficiency? Anyone who left behind that aura of fun and complicity? Sula never competed; she simply helped others define themselves. Other people seemed to turn their volume on and up when Sula was in the room. More than any other thing, humor returned. She could listen to the crunch of sugar underfoot that the children had spilled without reaching for the switch; and she forgot the tear in the living-room window shade. Even Nel's love for Jude, which over the years had spun a steady gray web around her heart, became a bright and easy affection, a playfulness that was reflected in their lovemaking.

Sula would come by of an afternoon, walking along with her fluid stride, wearing a plain yellow dress the same way her mother, Hannah, had worn those too-big house dresses — with a distance, an absence of a relationship to clothes which emphasized everything the fabric covered. When she scratched the screen door, as in the old days, and stepped inside, the dishes piled in the sink looked as though they belonged there; the dust on the lamps sparkled; the hair brush lying on the "good" sofa in the living room did not have to be apologetically retrieved, and Nel's grimy intractable children looked like three wild things happily insouciant in the May shine.

"Hey, girl." The rose mark over Sula's eye gave her glance a suggestion of startled pleasure. It was darker than Nel remembered.

"Hey yourself. Come on in here."

"How you doin'?" Sula moved a pile of ironed diapers from a chair and sat down.

"Oh, I ain't strangled nobody yet so I guess I'm all right."

"Well, if you change your mind call me."

"Somebody need killin'?"

"Half this town need it."

"And the other half?"

"A drawn-out disease."

"Oh, come on. Is Medallion that bad?"

"Didn't nobody tell you?"

"You been gone too long, Sula."

"Not too long, but maybe too far."

"What's that supposed to mean?" Nel

dipped her fingers into the bowl of water and sprinkled a diaper.

"Oh, I don't know."

"Want some cool tea?"

"Mmmm. Lots of ice, I'm burnin' up."

"Iceman don't come yet, but it's good and cold."

"That's fine."

"Hope I didn't speak too soon. Kids run in and out of here so much." Nel bent to open the icebox.

"You puttin' it on, Nel. Jude must be wore out."

"*Jude* must be wore out? You don't care nothin' 'bout my back, do you?"

"Is that where it's at, in your back?"

"Hah! Jude thinks it's everywhere."

"He's right, it is everywhere. Just be glad he found it, wherever it is. Remember John L.?"

"When Shirley said he got her down by the well and tried to stick it in her hip?" Nel giggled at the remembrance of that teen-time tale. "She should have been grateful. Have you seen her since you been back?"

"Mmm. Like a ox."

"That was one dumb nigger, John L."

"Maybe. Maybe he was just sanitary."

"Sanitary?"

"Well. Think about it. Suppose Shirley was all splayed out in front of you? Wouldn't you go for the hipbone instead?"

Nel lowered her head onto crossed arms while tears of laughter dripped into the warm diapers. Laughter that weakened her knees and pressed her bladder into action. Her rapid soprano and Sula's dark sleepy chuckle made a duet that frightened the cat and made the children run in from the back yard, puzzled at first by the wild free sounds, then delighted to see their mother stumbling merrily toward the bathroom, holding on to her stomach, fairly singing through the laughter: "Aw. Aw. Lord. Sula. Stop." And the other one, the one with the scary black thing over her eye, laughing softly and egging their mother on: "Neatness counts. You know what cleanliness is next to . . ."

"Hush." Nel's plea was clipped off by the slam of the bathroom door.

"What y'all laughing at?"

"Old time-y stuff. Long gone, old time-y stuff."

"Tell us."

"Tell *you?*" The black mark leaped.

"Uh huh. Tell us."

"What tickles us wouldn't tickle you."

"Uh huh, it would."

"Well, we was talking about some people we used to know when we was little."

"Was my mamma little?"

"Of course."

"What happened?"

"Well, some old boy we knew name John L. and a girl name . . ."

Damp-faced, Nel stepped back into the kitchen. She felt new, soft and new. It had been the longest time since she had had a rib-scraping laugh. She had forgotten how deep and down it could be. So different from the miscellaneous giggles and smiles she had learned to be content with these past few years.

"O Lord, Sula. You haven't changed none." She wiped her eyes. "What was all that about, anyway? All that scramblin' we did trying to do it and not do it at the same time?"

"Beats me. Such a simple thing."

"But we sure made a lot out of it, and the boys were dumber than we were."

"Couldn't nobody be dumber than I was."

"Stop lying. All of 'em liked you best."

"Yeah? Where are they?"

"They still here. You the one went off."

"Didn't I, though?"

"Tell me about it. The big city."

"Big is all it is. A big Medallion."

"No. I mean the life. The nightclubs, and parties . . ."

"I was in college, Nellie. No nightclubs on campus."

"Campus? That what they call it? Well. You wasn't in no college for — what — ten years now? And you didn't write to nobody. How come you never wrote?"

"You never did either."

"Where was I going to write to? All I knew was that you was in Nashville. I asked Miss Peace about you once or twice."

"What did *she* say?"

"I couldn't make much sense out of her. You know she been gettin' stranger and stranger after she come out the hospital. How is she anyway?"

"Same, I guess. Not so hot."

"No? Laura, I know, was doing her cooking and things. Is she still?"

"No. I put her out."

"Put her out? What for?"

"She made me nervous."

"But she was doing it for nothing, Sula."

"That's what you think. She was stealing right and left."

"Since when did you get froggy about folks' stealing?"

138

Sula smiled. "OK. I lied. You wanted a reason."

"Well, give me the real one."

"I don't know the real one. She just didn't belong in that house. Digging around in the cupboards, picking up pots and ice picks . . ."

"You sure have changed. That house was always full of people digging in cupboards and carrying on."

"That's the reason, then."

"Sula. Come on, now."

"You've changed too. I didn't used to have to explain everything to you."

Nel blushed. "Who's feeding the deweys and Tar Baby? You?"

"Sure me. Anyway Tar Baby don't eat and the deweys still crazy."

"I heard one of 'em's mamma came to take him back but didn't know which was hern."

"Don't nobody know."

"And Eva? You doing the work for her too?"

"Well, since you haven't heard it, let me tell you. Eva's real sick. I had her put where she could be watched and taken care of."

"Where would that be?"

"Out by Beechnut."

"You mean that home the white church run? Sula! That ain't no place for Eva. All them women is dirt poor with no people at all. Mrs. Wilkens and them. They got dropsy and can't hold their water — crazy as loons. Eva's odd, but she got sense. I don't think that's right, Sula."

"I'm scared of her, Nellie. That's why . . ."

"Scared? Of Eva?"

"You don't know her. Did you know she burnt Plum?"

"Oh, I heard that years ago. But nobody put no stock in it."

"They should have. It's true. I saw it. And when I got back here she was planning to do it to me too."

"Eva? I can't hardly believe that. She almost died trying to get to your mother."

Sula leaned forward, her elbows on the table. "You ever known me to lie to you?"

"No. But you could be mistaken. Why would Eva . . ."

"All I know is I'm scared. And there's no place else for me to go. We all that's left, Eva and me. I guess I should have stayed gone. I didn't know what else to do. Maybe I should have talked to you about it first. You always had better sense than me. Whenever I was scared before, you knew just what to do."

The closed place in the water spread before them. Nel put the iron on the stove. The situation was clear to her now. Sula, like always, was incapable of making any but the most trivial decisions. When it came to matters of grave importance, she behaved emotionally and irresponsibly and left it to others to straighten out. And when fear struck her, she did unbelievable things. Like that time with her finger. Whatever those hunkies did, it wouldn't have been as bad as what she did to herself. But Sula was so scared she had mutilated herself, to protect herself.

"What should I do, Nellie? Take her back and sleep with my door locked again?"

"No. I guess it's too late anyway. But let's work out a plan for taking care of her. So she won't be messed over."

"Anything you say."

"What about money? She got any?"

Sula shrugged. "The checks come still. It's not much, like it used to be. Should I have them made over to me?"

"Can you? Do it, then. We can arrange for her to have special comforts. That place is a mess, you know. A doctor don't never set foot in there. I ain't figured out yet how they stay alive in there as long as they do."

"Why don't I have the checks made over to you, Nellie? You better at this than I am."

"Oh no. People will say I'm scheming. You the one to do it. Was there insurance from Hannah?"

"Yes. Plum too. He had all that army insurance."

"Any of it left?"

"Well I went to college on some. Eva banked the rest. I'll look into it, though."

". . . and explain it all to the bank people."

"Will you go down with me?"

"Sure. It's going to be all right."

"I'm glad I talked to you 'bout this. It's been bothering me."

"Well, tongues will wag, but so long as we know the truth, it don't matter."

Just at that moment the children ran in announcing the entrance of their father. Jude opened the back door and walked into the kitchen. He was still a very good-looking man, and the only difference Sula could see was the thin pencil mustache under his nose, and a part in his hair.

"Hey, Jude. What you know good?"

"White man running it — nothing good."

Sula laughed while Nel, high-tuned to

his moods, ignored her husband's smile saying, "Bad day, honey?"

"Same old stuff," he replied and told them a brief tale of some personal insult done him by a customer and his boss — a whiney tale that peaked somewhere between anger and a lapping desire for comfort. He ended it with the observation that a Negro man had a hard row to hoe in this world. He expected his story to dovetail into milkwarm commiseration, but before Nel could excrete it, Sula said she didn't know about that — it looked like a pretty good life to her.

"Say what?" Jude's temper flared just a bit as he looked at this friend of his wife's, this slight woman, not exactly plain, but not fine either, with a copperhead over her eye. As far as he could tell, she looked like a woman roaming the country trying to find some man to burden down with a lot of lip and a lot of mouths.

Sula was smiling. "I mean, I don't know what the fuss is about. I mean, everything in the world loves you. White men love you. They spend so much time worrying about your penis they forget their own. The only thing they want to do is cut off a nigger's privates. And if that ain't love and respect I don't know what is. And white women? They chase you all to every corner of the earth, feel for you under every bed. I knew a white woman wouldn't leave the house after 6 o'clock for fear one of you would snatch her. Now ain't that love? They think rape soon's they see you, and if they don't get the rape they looking for, they scream it anyway just so the search won't be in vain. Colored women worry themselves into bad health just trying to hang on to your cuffs. Even little children — white and black, boys and girls — spend all their childhood eating their hearts out 'cause they think you don't love them. And if that ain't enough, you love yourselves. Nothing in this world loves a black man more than another black man. You hear of solitary white men, but niggers? Can't stay away from one another a whole day. So. It looks to me like you the envy of the world."

Jude and Nel were laughing, he saying, "Well, if that's the only way they got to show it — cut off my balls and throw me in jail — I'd just as soon they left me alone." But thinking that Sula had an odd way of looking at things and that her wide smile took some of the sting from that rattle-snake over her eye. A funny woman, he thought, not that bad-looking. But he could see why she wasn't married; she stirred a man's mind maybe, but not his body.

⬡⬡⬡

He left his tie. The one with the scriggly yellow lines running lopsided across the dark-blue field. It hung over the top of the closet door pointing steadily downward while it waited with every confidence for Jude to return.

Could he be gone if his tie is still here? He will remember it and come back and then she would . . . uh. Then she could . . . tell him. Sit down quietly and tell him. "But Jude," she would say, "you *knew* me. All those days and years, Jude, you *knew* me. My ways and my hands and how my stomach folded and how we tried to get Mickey to nurse and how about that time when the landlord said . . . but you said . . . and I cried, Jude. You knew me and had listened to the things I said in the night, and heard me in the bathroom and laughed at my raggedy girdle and I laughed too because I knew you too, Jude. So how could you leave me when you knew me?"

But they had been down on all fours naked, not touching except their lips right down there on the floor where the tie is pointing to, on all fours like (uh huh, go on, say it) like dogs. Nibbling at each other, not even touching, not even looking at each other, just their lips, and when I opened the door they didn't even look for a minute and I thought the reason they are not looking up is because they are not doing that. So it's all right. I am just standing here. They are not doing that. I am just standing here and seeing it, but they are not really doing it. But then they did look up. Or you did. You did, Jude. And if only you had not looked at me the way the soldiers did on the train, the way you look at the children when they come in while you are listening to Gabriel Heatter and break your train of thought — not focusing exactly but giving them an instant, a piece of time, to remember what they are doing, what they are interrupting, and to go on back to wherever they were and let you listen to Gabriel Heatter. And I did not know how to move my feet or fix my eyes or what. I just stood there seeing it and smiling, because maybe there was some explanation, something important that I did not know about that would have made it all right. I waited for Sula to look up at me any minute and say one of those lovely college words like *aesthetic* or *rap-*

port, which I never understood but which I loved because they sounded so comfortable and firm. And finally you just got up and started putting on your clothes and your privates were hanging down, so soft, and you buckled your pants belt but forgot to button the fly and she was sitting on the bed not even bothering to put on her clothes because actually she didn't need to because somehow she didn't look naked to me, only you did. Her chin was in her hand and she sat like a visitor from out of town waiting for the hosts to get some quarreling done and over with so the card game could continue and me wanting her to leave so I could tell you privately that you had forgotten to button your fly because I didn't want to say it in front of her, Jude. And even when you began to talk, I couldn't hear because I was worried about you not knowing that your fly was open and scared too because your eyes looked like the soldiers' that time on the train when my mother turned to custard.

Remember how big that bedroom was? Jude? How when we moved here we said, Well, at least we got us a real big bedroom, but it was small then, Jude, and so shambly, and maybe it was that way all along but it would have been better if I had gotten the dust out from under the bed because I was ashamed of it in that small room. And then you walked past me saying, "I'll be back for my things." And you did but you left your tie.

The clock was ticking. Nel looked at it and realized that it was two thirty, only forty-five minutes before the children would be home and she hadn't even felt anything right or sensible and now there was no time or wouldn't be until nighttime when they were asleep and she could get into bed and maybe she could do it then. Think. But who could think in that bed where *they* had been and where they *also* had been and where only she was now?

She looked around for a place to be. A small place. The closet? No. Too dark. The bathroom. It was both small and bright, and she wanted to be in a very small, very bright place. Small enough to contain her grief. Bright enough to throw into relief the dark things that cluttered her. Once inside, she sank to the tile floor next to the toilet. On her knees, her hand on the cold rim of the bathtub, she waited for something to happen . . . inside. There was stirring, a movement of mud and dead leaves. She thought of the women at Chicken Little's funeral. The women who shrieked over the bier and at the lip of the open grave. What she had regarded since as unbecoming behavior seemed fitting to her now; they were screaming at the neck of God, his giant nape, the vast back-of-the-head that he had turned on them in death. But it seemed to her now that it was not a fist-shaking grief they were keening but rather a simple obligation to say something, do something, feel something about the dead. They could not let that heart-smashing event pass unrecorded, unidentified. It was poisonous, unnatural to let the dead go with a mere whimpering, a slight murmur, a rose bouquet of good taste. Good taste was out of place in the company of death, death itself was the essence of bad taste. And there must be much rage and saliva in its presence. The body must move and throw itself about, the eyes must roll, the hands should have no peace, and the throat should release all the yearning, despair and outrage that accompany the stupidity of loss.

"The real hell of Hell is that it is forever." Sula said that. She said doing anything forever and ever was hell. Nel didn't understand it then, but now in the bathroom, trying to feel, she thought, "If I could be sure that I could stay here in this small white room with the dirty tile and water gurgling in the pipes and my head on the cool rim of this bathtub and never have to go out the door, I would be happy. If I could be certain that I never had to get up and flush the toilet, go in the kitchen, watch my children grow up and die, see my food chewed on my plate . . . Sula was wrong. Hell ain't things lasting forever. Hell is change." Not only did men leave and children grow up and die, but even the misery didn't last. One day she wouldn't even have that. This very grief that had twisted her into a curve on the floor and flayed her would be gone. She would lose that too.

"Why, even in hate here I am thinking of what Sula said."

Hunched down in the small bright room Nel waited. Waited for the oldest cry. A scream not for others, not in sympathy for a burnt child, or a dead father, but a deeply personal cry for one's own pain. A loud, strident: "Why me?" She waited. The mud shifted, the leaves stirred, the smell of overripe green things enveloped her and announced the beginnings of her very own howl.

But it did not come.

The odor evaporated; the leaves were still, the mud settled. And finally there was nothing, just a flake of something dry and nasty in her throat. She stood up frightened. There was something just to the right of her, in the air, just out of view. She could not see it, but she knew exactly what it looked like. A gray ball hovering just there. Just there. To the right. Quiet, gray, dirty. A ball of muddy strings, but without weight, fluffy but terrible in its malevolence. She knew she could not look, so she closed her eyes and crept past it out of the bathroom, shutting the door behind her. Sweating with fear, she stepped to the kitchen door and onto the back porch. The lilac bushes preened at the railing, but there were no lilacs yet. Wasn't it time? Surely it was time. She looked over the fence to Mrs. Rayford's yard. Hers were not in bloom either. Was it too late? She fastened on this question with enthusiasm, all the time aware of something she was not thinking. It was the only way she could get her mind off the flake in her throat.

She spent a whole summer with the gray ball, the little ball of fur and string and hair always floating in the light near her but which she did not see because she never looked. But that was the terrible part, the effort it took not to look. But it was there anyhow, just to the right of her head and maybe further down by her shoulder, so when the children went to a monster movie at the Elmira Theater and came home and said, "Mamma, can you sleep with us tonight?" she said all right and got into bed with the two boys, who loved it, but the girl did not. For a long time she could not stop getting in the bed with her children and told herself each time that they might dream a dream about dragons and would need her to comfort them. It was so nice to think about their scary dreams and not about a ball of fur. She even hoped their dreams would rub off on her and give her the wonderful relief of a nightmare so she could stop going around scared to turn her head this way or that lest she see it. That was the scary part — seeing it. It was not coming at her; it never did that, or tried to pounce on her. It just floated there for the seeing, if she wanted to, and O my God for the touching if she wanted to. But she didn't want to see it, ever, for if she saw it, who could tell but what she might actually touch it, or want to, and then what would happen if she actually reached out her hand and touched it? Die probably, but no worse than that.

Dying was OK because it was sleep and there wasn't no gray ball in death, was there? Was there? She would have to ask somebody about that, somebody she could confide in and who knew a lot of things, like Sula, for Sula would know or if she didn't she would say something funny that would make it all right. Ooo no, not Sula. Here she was in the midst of it, hating it, scared of it, and again she thought of Sula as though they were still friends and talked things over. That was too much. To lose Jude and not have Sula to talk to about it because it was Sula that he had left her for.

Now her thighs were really empty. And it was then that what those women said about never looking at another man made some sense to her, for the real point, the heart of what they said, was the word *looked*. Not to promise never to make love to another man, not to refuse to marry another man, but to promise and know that she could never afford to look again, to see and accept the way in which their heads cut the air or see moons and tree limbs framed by their necks and shoulders . . . never to look, for now she could not risk looking — and anyway, so what? For now her thighs were truly empty and dead too, and it was Sula who had taken the life

153

from them and Jude who smashed her heart and the both of them who left her with no thighs and no heart just her brain raveling away.

And what am I supposed to do with these old thighs now, just walk up and down these rooms? What good are they, Jesus? They will never give me the peace I need to get from sunup to sundown, what good are they, are you trying to tell me that I am going to have to go all the way through these days all the way, O my god, to that box with four handles with never nobody settling down between my legs even if I sew up those old pillow cases and rinse down the porch and feed my children and beat the rugs and haul the coal up out of the bin even then nobody, O Jesus, I could be a mule or plow the furrows with my hands if need be or hold these rickety walls up with my back if need be if I knew that somewhere in this world in the pocket of some night I could open my legs to some cowboy lean hips but you are trying to tell me no and O my sweet Jesus what kind of cross is that?

1939

When the word got out about Eva being put in Sunnydale, the people in the Bottom shook their heads and said Sula was a roach. Later, when they saw how she took Jude, then ditched him for others, and heard how he bought a bus ticket to Detroit (where he bought but never mailed birthday cards to his sons), they forgot all about Hannah's easy ways (or their own) and said she was a bitch. Everybody remembered the plague of robins that announced her return, and the tale about her watching Hannah burn was stirred up again.

But it was the men who gave her the final label, who fingerprinted her for all time. They were the ones who said she was guilty of the unforgivable thing — the thing for which there was no under-standing, no excuse, no compassion. The route from which there was no way back, the dirt that could not ever be washed away. They said that Sula slept with white men. It may not have been true, but it certainly could have been. She was obviously capable of it. In any case, all minds were closed to her when that word was passed around. It made the old women draw their lips together; made small children look away from her in shame; made young men fantasize elaborate torture for her — just to get the saliva back in their mouths when they saw her.

Every one of them imagined the scene, each according to his own predilections — Sula underneath some white man — and it filled them with choking disgust. There was nothing lower she could do, nothing filthier. The fact that their own skin color was proof that it had happened in their own families was no deterrent to their bile. Nor was the willingness of black men to lie in the beds of white women a consideration that might lead them toward tolerance. They insisted that all unions between white men and black women be rape; for a black woman to be willing was literally unthinkable. In that way, they regarded integration with precisely the same venom that white people did.

So they laid broomsticks across their doors at night and sprinkled salt on porch steps. But aside from one or two unsuccessful efforts to collect the dust from her footsteps, they did nothing to harm her. As always the black people looked at evil stony-eyed and let it run.

Sula acknowledged none of their attempts at counter-conjure or their gossip and seemed to need the services of nobody. So they watched her far more closely than they watched any other roach or bitch in the town, and their alertness was gratified. Things began to happen.

First off, Teapot knocked on her door to see if she had any bottles. He was the five-year-old son of an indifferent mother, all of whose interests sat around the door of the Time and a Half Pool Hall. Her name was Betty but she was called Teapot's Mamma because being his mamma was precisely her major failure. When Sula said no, the boy turned around and fell down the steps. He couldn't get up right away and Sula went to help him. His mother, just then tripping home, saw Sula bending over her son's pained face. She flew into a fit of concerned, if drunken, motherhood, and dragged Teapot home. She told everybody that Sula had pushed him, and talked so strongly about it she was forced to abide by the advice of her friends and take him to the county hospital. The two dollars she hated to release turned out to be well spent, for Teapot did have a fracture, although the doctor said poor diet had contributed substantially to the daintiness of his bones. Teapot's Mamma got a lot of attention anyway and immersed herself in a role she had shown no inclination for: motherhood. The very idea of a grown woman hurting her boy kept her teeth on edge. She became the most devoted mother: sober, clean and industrious. No more nickels for Teapot to go to Dick's for a breakfast of Mr. Goodbars and soda pop: no more long hours of him alone or wandering the roads while she was otherwise engaged. Her change was a distinct improvement, although little Teapot did miss those quiet times at Dick's.

Other things happened. Mr. Finley sat on his porch sucking chicken bones, as he had done for thirteen years, looked up, saw Sula, choked on a bone and died on the spot. That incident, and Teapot's Mamma, cleared up for everybody the meaning of the birthmark over her eye; it was not a stemmed rose, or a snake, it was Hannah's ashes marking her from the very beginning.

She came to their church suppers

without underwear, bought their steaming platters of food and merely picked at it — relishing nothing, exclaiming over no one's ribs or cobbler. They believed that she was laughing at their God.

And the fury she created in the women of the town was incredible — for she would lay their husbands once and then no more. Hannah had been a nuisance, but she was complimenting the women, in a way, by wanting their husbands. Sula was trying them out and discarding them without any excuse the men could swallow. So the women, to justify their own judgment, cherished their men more, soothed the pride and vanity Sula had bruised.

Among the weighty evidence piling up was the fact that Sula did not look her age. She was near thirty and, unlike them, had lost no teeth, suffered no bruises, developed no ring of fat at the waist or pocket at the back of her neck. It was rumored that she had had no childhood diseases, was never known to have chicken pox, croup or even a runny nose. She had played rough as a child — where were the scars? Except for a funny-shaped finger and that evil birthmark, she was free of any normal signs of vulnerability. Some of the men, who as boys had dated her, remembered

that on picnics neither gnats nor mosqui-
toes would settle on her. Patsy, Hannah's
one-time friend, agreed and said not only
that, but she had witnessed the fact that
when Sula drank beer she never belched.

The most damning evidence, however,
came from Dessie, who was a big Daughter
Elk and knew things. At one of the social
meetings she revealed something to her
friends.

"Yeh, well I noticed something long time
ago. Ain't said nothing 'bout it 'cause I
wasn't sure what it meant. Well . . . I did
mention it to Ivy but not nobody else. I
disremember how long ago. 'Bout a month
or two I guess 'cause I hadn't put down my
new linoleum yet. Did you see it, Cora? It's
that kind we saw in the catalogue."

"Naw."

"Get on with it, Dessie."

"Well, Cora was with me when we
looked in the catalogue . . ."

"We all know 'bout your linoleum. What
we don't know is . . ."

"OK. Let me tell it, will you? Just before
the linoleum come I was out front and
seed Shadrack carryin' on as usual . . . up
by the well . . . walkin' 'round it salutin'
and carryin' on. You know how he does . . .
hollerin' commands and . . ."

"Will you get on with it?"

"Who's tellin' this? Me or you?"

"You."

"Well, let me tell it then. Like I say, he was just cuttin' up as usual when Miss Sula Mae walks by on the other side of the road. And quick as that" — she snapped her fingers — "he stopped and cut on over 'cross the road, steppin' over to her like a tall turkey in short corn. And guess what? He tips his hat."

"Shadrack don't wear no hat."

"I know that but he tipped it anyway. You know what I mean. He acted like he had a hat and reached up for it and tipped it at her. Now you know Shadrack ain't civil to nobody!"

"Sure ain't."

"Even when you buyin' his fish he's cussin'. If you ain't got the right change he cussin' you. If you act like a fish ain't too fresh he snatch it out of your hand like he doin' you the favor."

"Well, everybody know he a reprobate."

"Yeh, so how come he tip his hat to Sula? How come he don't cuss her?"

"Two devils."

"Exactly!"

"What'd she do when he tipped it? Smile and give him a curtsey?"

161

"No, and that was the other thing. It was the first time I see her look anything but hateful. Like she smellin' you with her eyes and don't like your soap. When he tipped his hat she put her hand on her throat for a minute and *cut* out. Went runnin' on up the road to home. And him still standin' there tippin' away. And — this the point I was comin' to — when I went back in the house a big sty come on my eye. And I ain't never had no sty before. Never!"

"That's 'cause you saw it."

"Exactly."

"Devil all right."

"No two ways about it," Dessie said, and she popped the rubber band off the deck of cards to settle them down for a nice long game of bid whist.

Their conviction of Sula's evil changed them in accountable yet mysterious ways. Once the source of their personal misfortune was identified, they had leave to protect and love one another. They began to cherish their husbands and wives, protect their children, repair their homes and in general band together against the devil in their midst. In their world, aberrations were as much a part of nature as grace. It was not for them to expel or annihilate it.

162

They would no more run Sula out of town than they would kill the robins that brought her back, for in their secret awareness of Him, He was not the God of three faces they sang about. They knew quite well that He had four, and that the fourth explained Sula. They had lived with various forms of evil all their days, and it wasn't that they believed God would take care of them. It was rather that they knew God had a brother and that brother hadn't spared God's son, so why should he spare them?

There was no creature so ungodly as to make them destroy it. They could kill easily if provoked to anger, but not by design, which explained why they could not "mob kill" anyone. To do so was not only unnatural, it was undignified. The presence of evil was something to be first recognized, then dealt with, survived, outwitted, triumphed over.

Their evidence against Sula was contrived, but their conclusions about her were not. Sula was distinctly different. Eva's arrogance and Hannah's self-indulgence merged in her and, with a twist that was all her own imagination, she lived out her days exploring her own thoughts and emotions, giving them full reign, feeling no obligation to please anybody unless their pleasure pleased her. As willing to feel pain as to give pain, to feel pleasure as to give pleasure, hers was an experimental life — ever since her mother's remarks sent her flying up those stairs, ever since her one major feeling of responsibility had been exorcised on the bank of a river with a closed place in the middle. The first experience taught her there was no other that you could count on; the second that there was no self to count on either. She had no center, no speck around which to grow. In the midst of a pleasant conversation with someone she might say, "Why do you chew with your mouth open?" not because the answer interested her but because she wanted to see the person's face change rapidly. She was completely free of ambition, with no affection for money, property or things, no greed, no desire to command attention or compliments — no ego. For that reason she felt no compulsion to verify herself — be consistent with herself.

She had clung to Nel as the closest thing to both an other and a self, only to discover that she and Nel were not one and the same thing. She had no thought at all of causing Nel pain when she bedded down with Jude. They had always shared the affection of other people: compared how a boy kissed, what line he used with one and then the other. Marriage, apparently, had changed all that, but having had no intimate knowledge of marriage, having lived in a house with women who thought all men available, and selected from among them with a care only for their tastes, she was ill prepared for the possessiveness of the one person she felt close to. She knew well enough what other women said and felt, or said they felt. But she and Nel had always seen through them. They both knew that those women were not jealous of other women; that they were only afraid of losing their jobs. Afraid their husbands would discover that no uniqueness lay between their legs.

Nel was the one person who had wanted nothing from her, who had accepted all aspects of her. Now she wanted everything, and all because of *that*. Nel was the first person who had been real to her, whose name she knew, who had seen as she had the slant of life that made it possible to stretch it to its limits. Now Nel was one of *them*. One of the spiders whose only thought was the next rung of the web, who dangled in dark dry places suspended by their own spittle, more terrified of the free fall than the snake's breath below. Their eyes so intent on the wayward stranger who trips into their net, they were blind to the cobalt on their own backs, the moonshine fighting to pierce their corners. If they were touched by the snake's breath, however fatal, they were merely victims and knew how to behave in that role (just as Nel knew how to behave as the wronged wife). But the free fall, oh no, that required — demanded — invention: a thing to do with the wings, a way of holding the legs and most of all a full surrender to the downward flight if they wished to taste their tongues or stay alive. But alive was what they, and now Nel, did not want to be. Too dangerous. Now Nel belonged to the town and all of its ways. She had given herself over to them, and the flick of their tongues would drive her back into her little dry corner where she would cling to her spittle high above the breath of the snake and the fall.

It had surprised her a little and saddened her a good deal when Nel behaved the way the others would have. Nel was one of the reasons she had drifted back to Medallion, that and the boredom she found in Nashville, Detroit, New Orleans, New York, Philadelphia, Macon and San

Diego. All those cities held the same people, working the same mouths, sweating the same sweat. The men who took her to one or another of those places had merged into one large personality: the same language of love, the same entertainments of love, the same cooling of love. Whenever she introduced her private thoughts into their rubbings or goings, they hooded their eyes. They taught her nothing but love tricks, shared nothing but worry, gave nothing but money. She had been looking all along for a friend, and it took her a while to discover that a lover was not a comrade and could never be — for a woman. And that no one would ever be that version of herself which she sought to reach out to and touch with an ungloved hand. There was only her own mood and whim, and if that was all there was, she decided to turn the naked hand toward it, discover it and let others become as intimate with their own selves as she was.

In a way, her strangeness, her naïveté, her craving for the other half of her equation was the consequence of an idle imagination. Had she paints, or clay, or knew the discipline of the dance, or strings; had she anything to engage her tremendous curiosity and her gift for metaphor, she might have exchanged the restlessness and preoccupation with whim for an activity that provided her with all she yearned for. And like any artist with no art form, she became dangerous.

She had lied only once in her life — to Nel about the reason for putting Eva out, and she could lie to her only because she cared about her. When she had come back home, social conversation was impossible for her because she could not lie. She could not say to those old acquaintances, "Hey, girl, you looking good," when she saw how the years had dusted their bronze with ash, the eyes that had once opened wide to the moon bent into grimy sickles of concern. The narrower their lives, the wider their hips. Those with husbands had folded themselves into starched coffins, their sides bursting with other people's skinned dreams and bony regrets. Those without men were like sour-tipped needles featuring one constant empty eye. Those with men had had the sweetness sucked from their breath by ovens and steam kettles. Their children were like distant but exposed wounds whose aches were no less intimate because separate from their flesh. They had looked at the world and back at their children, back at the world and back again at their children, and Sula knew that one clear young eye was all that kept the knife away from the throat's curve.

She was pariah, then, and knew it. Knew that they despised her and believed that they framed their hatred as disgust for the easy way she lay with men. Which was true. She went to bed with men as frequently as she could. It was the only place where she could find what she was looking for: misery and the ability to feel deep sorrow. She had not always been aware that it was sadness that she yearned for. Lovemaking seemed to her, at first, the creation of a special kind of joy. She thought she liked the sootiness of sex and its comedy; she laughed a great deal during the raucous beginnings, and rejected those lovers who regarded sex as healthy or beautiful. Sexual aesthetics bored her. Although she did not regard sex as ugly (ugliness was boring also), she liked to think of it as wicked. But as her experiences multiplied she realized that not only was it not wicked, it was not necessary for her to conjure up the idea of wickedness in order to participate fully. During the lovemaking she found and needed to find the cutting edge. When she left off cooperating with her body and began to assert herself in the act, particles of strength gathered in her like steel shavings drawn to a spacious magnetic center, forming a tight cluster that nothing, it seemed, could break. And there was utmost irony and outrage in lying under someone, in a position of surrender, feeling her own abiding strength and limitless power. But the cluster did break, fall apart, and in her panic to hold it together she leaped from the edge into soundlessness and went down howling, howling in a stinging awareness of the endings of things: an eye of sorrow in the midst of all that hurricane rage of joy. There, in the center of that silence was not eternity but the death of time and a loneliness so profound the word itself had no meaning. For loneliness assumed the absence of other people, and the solitude she found in that desperate terrain had never admitted the possibility of other people. She wept then. Tears for the deaths of the littlest things: the castaway shoes of children; broken stems of marsh grass battered and drowned by the sea; prom photographs of dead women she never knew; wedding rings in pawnshop windows; the tidy bodies of Cornish hens in a nest of rice.

When her partner disengaged himself,

she looked up at him in wonder trying to recall his name; and he looked down at her, smiling with tender understanding of the state of tearful gratitude to which he believed he had brought her. She waiting impatiently for him to turn away and settle into a wet skim of satisfaction and light disgust, leaving her to the postcoital privateness in which she met herself, welcomed herself, and joined herself in matchless harmony.

At twenty-nine she knew it would be no other way for her, but she had not counted on the footsteps on the porch, and the beautiful black face that stared at her through the blue-glass window. Ajax.

Looking for all the world as he had seventeen years ago when he had called her pig meat. He was twenty-one then, she twelve. A universe of time between them. Now she was twenty-nine, he thirty-eight, and the lemon-yellow haunches seemed not so far away after all.

She opened the heavy door and saw him standing on the other side of the screen door with two quarts of milk tucked into his arms like marble statues. He smiled and said, "I been lookin' all over for you."

"Why?" she asked.

"To give you these," and he nodded toward one of the quarts of milk.

"I don't like milk," she said.

"But you like bottles don't you?" He held one up. "Ain't that pretty?"

And indeed it was. Hanging from his fingers, framed by a slick blue sky, it looked precious and clean and permanent. She had the distinct impression that he had done something dangerous to get them.

Sula ran her fingernails over the screen thoughtfully for a second and then, laughing, she opened the screen door.

Ajax came in and headed straight for the kitchen. Sula followed slowly. By the time she got to the door he had undone the complicated wire cap and was letting the cold milk run into his mouth.

Sula watched him — or rather the rhythm in his throat — with growing interest. When he had had enough, he poured the rest into the sink, rinsed the bottle out and presented it to her. She took the bottle with one hand and his wrist with the other and pulled him into the pantry. There was no need to go there, for not a soul was in the house, but the gesture came to Hannah's daughter naturally. There in the pantry, empty now of flour sacks, void of row upon row of canned goods, free forever of strings of tiny green peppers, holding the wet milk bottle tight in her arm she stood wide-legged against the wall and pulled from his track-lean hips all the pleasure her thighs could hold.

He came regularly then, bearing gifts: clusters of blackberries still on their branches, four meal-fried porgies wrapped in a salmon-colored sheet of the Pittsburgh *Courier*, a handful of jacks, two boxes of lime Jell-Well, a hunk of ice-wagon ice, a can of Old Dutch Cleanser with the bonneted woman chasing dirt with her stick; a page of Tillie the Toiler comics, and more gleaming white bottles of milk.

Contrary to what anybody would have suspected from just seeing him lounging around the pool hall, or shooting at Mr. Finley for beating his own dog, or calling filthy compliments to passing women, Ajax was very nice to women. His women, of course, knew it, and it provoked them into murderous battles over him in the streets, brawling thick-thighed women with knives disturbed many a Friday night with their bloodletting and attracted whooping crowds. On such occasions Ajax stood, along with the crowd, and viewed the fighters with the same golden-eyed indifference with which he watched old men playing checkers. Other than his mother, who sat in her shack with six younger sons working roots, he had never met an interesting woman in his life.

His kindness to them in general was not due to a ritual of seduction (he had no need for it) but rather to the habit he acquired in dealing with his mother, who inspired thoughtfulness and generosity in all her sons.

She was an evil conjure woman, blessed with seven adoring children whose joy it was to bring her the plants, hair, underclothing, fingernail parings, white hens, blood, camphor, pictures, kerosene and footstep dust that she needed, as well as to order Van Van, High John the Conqueror, Little John to Chew, Devil's Shoe String, Chinese Wash, Mustard Seed and the Nine Herbs from Cincinnati. She knew about the weather, omens, the living, the dead, dreams and all illnesses and made a modest living with her skills. Had she any teeth or ever straightened her back, she would have been the most gorgeous thing alive, worthy of her sons' worship for her beauty alone, if not for the absolute freedom she allowed them (known in some quarters as neglect) and the weight of her hoary knowledge.

This woman Ajax loved, and after her — airplanes. There was nothing in between. And when he was not sitting enchanted listening to his mother's words, he thought of airplanes, and pilots, and the deep sky that held them both. People thought that those long trips he took to large cities in the state were for some sophisticated good times they could not imagine but only envy; actually he was leaning against the barbed wire of airports, or nosing around hangars just to hear the talk of the men who were fortunate enough to be in the trade. The rest of the time, the time he was not watching his mother's magic or thinking of airplanes, he spent in the idle pursuits of bachelors without work in small towns. He had heard all the stories about Sula, and they aroused his curiosity. Her elusiveness and indifference to established habits of behavior reminded him of his mother, who was as stubborn in her pursuits of the occult as the women of Greater Saint Matthew's were in the search for redeeming grace. So when his curiosity was high enough he picked two bottles of milk off the porch of some white family and went to see her, suspecting that this was perhaps the only other woman he knew whose life was her own, who could deal with life efficiently, and who was not interested in nailing him.

Sula, too, was curious. She knew nothing about him except the word he had called out to her years ago and the feeling he had excited in her then. She had grown quite accustomed to the clichés of other people's lives as well as her own increasing dissatisfaction with Medallion. If she could have thought of a place to go, she probably would have left, but that was before Ajax looked at her through the blue glass and held the milk aloft like a trophy.

But it was not the presents that made her wrap him up in her thighs. They were charming, of course (especially the jar of butterflies he let loose in the bedroom), but her real pleasure was the fact that he talked to her. They had genuine conversations. He did not speak down to her or at her, nor content himself with puerile questions about her life or monologues of his own activities. Thinking she was possibly brilliant, like his mother, he seemed to expect brilliance from her, and she delivered. And in all of it, he listened more than he spoke. His clear comfort at being in her presence, his lazy willingness to tell her all about fixes and the powers of plants, his refusal to baby or protect her, his assump-

tion that she was both tough and wise —
all of that coupled with a wide generosity
of spirit only occasionally erupting into
vengeance sustained Sula's interest and enthusiasm.

His idea of bliss (on earth as opposed to
bliss in the sky) was a long bath in piping-
hot water — his head on the cool white
rim, his eyes closed in reverie.

"Soaking in hot water give you a bad
back." Sula stood in the doorway looking
at his knees glistening just at the surface of
the soap-gray water.

"Soaking in Sula give me a bad back."

"Worth it?"

"Don't know yet. Go 'way."

"Airplanes?"

"Airplanes."

"Lindbergh know about you?"

"Go 'way."

She went and waited for him in Eva's
high bed, her head turned to the boarded-
up window. She was smiling, thinking how
like Jude's was his craving to do the white
man's work, when two deweys came in
with their beautiful teeth and said, "We
sick."

Sula turned her head slowly and murmured, "Get well."

"We need some medicine."

"Look in the bathroom."

"Ajax in there."

"Then wait."

"We sick now."

Sula leaned over the bed, picked up a shoe and threw it at them.

"Cocksucker!" they screamed, and she leaped out of the bed naked as a yard dog. She caught the redheaded dewey by his shirt and held him by the heels over the banister until he wet his pants. The other dewey was joined by the third, and they delved into their pockets for stones, which they threw at her. Sula, ducking and tottering with laughter, carried the wet dewey to the bedroom and when the other two followed her, deprived of all weapons except their teeth, Sula had dropped the first dewey on the bed and was fishing in her purse. She gave each of them a dollar bill which they snatched and then scooted off down the stairs to Dick's to buy the catarrh remedy they loved to drink.

Ajax came sopping wet into the room and lay down on the bed to let the air dry him. They were both still for a long time until he reached out and touched her arm.

He liked for her to mount him so he could see her towering above him and call soft obscenities up into her face. As she rocked there, swayed there, like a Georgia pine on its knees, high above the slipping, falling smile, high above the golden eyes and the velvet helmet of hair, rocking, swaying, she focused her thoughts to bar the creeping disorder that was flooding her hips. She looked down, down from what seemed an awful height at the head of the man whose lemon-yellow gabardines had been the first sexual excitement she'd known. Letting her thoughts dwell on his face in order to confine, for just a while longer, the drift of her flesh toward the high silence of orgasm.

If I take a chamois and rub real hard on the bone, right on the ledge of your cheek bone, some of the black will disappear. It will flake away into the chamois and underneath there will be gold leaf. I can see it shining through the black. I know it is there . . .

How high she was over his wand-lean body, how slippery was his sliding sliding smile.

And if I take a nail file or even Eva's old paring knife — that will do — and scrape away at the gold, it will fall away and there will be alabaster. The alabaster is what gives your face its planes, its curves. That is why your mouth smiling does not reach your eyes. Alabaster is giving it a gravity that resists a total smile.

The height and the swaying dizzied her, so she bent down and let her breasts graze his chest.

Then I can take a chisel and small tap hammer and tap away at the alabaster. It will crack then like ice under the pick, and through the breaks I will see the loam, fertile, free of pebbles and twigs. For it is the loam that is giving you that smell.

She slipped her hands under his armpits, for it seemed as though she would not be able to dam the spread of weakness she felt under her skin without holding on to something.

I will put my hand deep into your soil, lift it, sift it with my fingers, feel its warm surface and dewy chill below.

She put her head under his chin with no hope in the world of keeping anything at all at bay.

I will water your soil, keep it rich and moist. But how much? How much water to keep the loam moist? And how much loam will I need to keep my water still? And when do the two make mud?

He swallowed her mouth just as her thighs had swallowed his genitals, and the house was very, very quiet.

⬡⬡⬡

Sula began to discover what possession

was. Not love, perhaps, but possession or at least the desire for it. She was astounded by so new and alien a feeling. First there was the morning of the night before when she actually wondered if Ajax would come by that day. Then there was an afternoon when she stood before the mirror finger-tracing the laugh lines around her mouth and trying to decide whether she was good-looking or not. She ended this deep perusal by tying a green ribbon in her hair. The green silk made a rippling whisper as she slid it into her hair — a whisper that could easily have been Hannah's chuckle, a soft slow nasal hiss she used to emit when something amused her. Like women sitting for two hours under the marcelling irons only to wonder two days later how soon they would need another appointment. The ribbon-tying was followed by other ac-tivity, and when Ajax came that evening, bringing her a reed whistle he had carved that morning, not only was the green ribbon still in her hair, but the bathroom was gleaming, the bed was made, and the table was set for two.

He gave her the reed whistle, unlaced his shoes and sat in the rocking chair in the kitchen.

Sula walked toward him and kissed his

mouth. He ran his fingers along the nape of her neck.

"I bet you ain't even missed Tar Baby, have you?" he asked.

"Missed? No. Where is he?"

Ajax smiled at her delicious indifference. "Jail."

"Since when?"

"Last Saturday."

"Picked up for drunk?"

"Little bit more than that," he answered and went ahead to tell her about his own involvement in another of Tar Baby's misfortunes.

On Saturday afternoon Tar Baby had stumbled drunk into traffic on the New River Road. A woman driver swerved to avoid him and hit another car. When the police came, they recognized the woman as the mayor's niece and arrested Tar Baby. Later, after the word got out, Ajax and two other men went to the station to see about him. At first they wouldn't let them in. But they relented after Ajax and the other two just stood around for one hour and a half and repeated their request at regular intervals. When they finally got permission to go in and looked in at him in the cell, he was twisted up in a corner badly beaten and dressed in nothing but extremely soiled underwear. Ajax and the other men asked the officer why Tar Baby couldn't have back his clothes. "It ain't right," they said, "to let a grown man lay around in his own shit."

The policeman, obviously in agreement with Eva, who had always maintained that Tar Baby was white, said that if the prisoner didn't like to live in shit, he should come down out of those hills, and live like a decent white man.

More words were exchanged, hot words and dark, and the whole thing ended with the arraignment of the three black men, and an appointment to appear in civil court Thursday next.

Ajax didn't seem too bothered by any of it. More annoyed and inconvenienced than anything else. He had had several messes with the police, mostly in gambling raids, and regarded them as the natural hazards of Negro life.

But Sula, the green ribbon shining in her hair, was flooded with an awareness of the impact of the outside world on Ajax. She stood up and arranged herself on the arm of the rocking chair. Putting her fingers deep into the velvet of his hair, she murmured, "Come on. Lean on me."

Ajax blinked. Then he looked swiftly

into her face. In her words, in her voice, was a sound he knew well. For the first time he saw the green ribbon. He looked around and saw the gleaming kitchen and the table set for two and detected the scent of the nest. Every hackle on his body rose, and he knew that very soon she would, like all of her sisters before her, put to him the death-knell question "Where you been?" His eyes dimmed with a mild and momentary regret.

He stood and mounted the stairs with her and entered the spotless bathroom where the dust had been swept from underneath the claw-foot tub. He was trying to remember the date of the air show in Dayton. As he came into the bedroom, he saw Sula lying on fresh white sheets, wrapped in the deadly odor of freshly applied cologne.

He dragged her under him and made love to her with the steadiness and the intensity of a man about to leave for Dayton.

Every now and then she looked around for tangible evidence of his having ever been there. Where were the butterflies? the blueberries? the whistling reed? She could find nothing, for he had left nothing but his stunning absence. An absence so decorative, so ornate, it was difficult for her to understand how she had ever endured, without falling dead or being consumed, his magnificent presence.

The mirror by the door was not a mirror by the door, it was an altar where he stood for only a moment to put on his cap before going out. The red rocking chair was a rocking of his own hips as he sat in the kitchen. Still, there was nothing of his — his own — that she could find. It was as if she were afraid she had hallucinated him and needed proof to the contrary. His absence was everywhere, stinging everything, giving the furnishings primary colors, sharp outlines to the corners of rooms and gold light to the dust collecting on table tops. When he was there he pulled everything toward himself. Not only her eyes and all her senses but also inanimate things seemed to exist because of him, backdrops to his presence. Now that he had gone, these things, so long subdued by his presence, were glamorized in his wake.

Then one day, burrowing in a dresser drawer, she found what she had been looking for: proof that he had been there, his driver's license. It contained just what she needed for verification — his vital statistics: Born 1901, height 5'11", weight

152 lbs., eyes brown, hair black, color black. Oh yes, skin black. Very black. So black that only a steady careful rubbing with steel wool would remove it, and as it was removed there was the glint of gold leaf and under the gold leaf the cold alabaster and deep, deep down under the cold alabaster more black only this time the black of warm loam.

But what was this? Albert Jacks? His name was Albert Jacks? A. Jacks. She had thought it was Ajax. All those years. Even from the time she walked by the pool hall and looked away from him sitting astride a wooden chair, looked away to keep from seeing the wide space of intolerable orderliness between his legs; the openness that held no sign, no sign at all, of the animal that lurked in his trousers; looked away from the insolent nostrils and the smile that kept slipping and falling, falling, falling so she wanted to reach out with her hand to catch it before it fell to the pavement and was sullied by the cigarette butts and bottle caps and spittle at his feet and the feet of other men who sat or stood around outside the pool hall, calling, singing out to her and Nel and grown women too with lyrics like *pig meat* and *brown sugar* and *jailbait* and *O Lord, what have I done to deserve the wrath,* and *Take me, Jesus, I have seen the promised land,* and *Do, Lord, remember me* in voices mellowed by hopeless passion into gentleness. Even then, when she and Nel were trying hard not to dream of him and not to think of him when they touched the softness in their underwear or undid their braids as soon as they left home to let the hair bump and wave around their ears, or wrapped the cotton binding around their chests so the nipples would not break through their blouses and give him cause to smile his slipping, falling smile, which brought the blood rushing to their skin. And even later, when for the first time in her life she had lain in bed with a man and said his name involuntarily or said it truly meaning *him,* the name she was screaming and saying was not his at all.

Sula stood with a worn slip of paper in her fingers and said aloud to no one, "I didn't even know his name. And if I didn't know his name, then there is nothing I did know and I have known nothing ever at all since the one thing I wanted was to know his name so how could he help but leave me since he was making love to a woman who didn't even know his name.

"When I was a little girl the heads of my

paper dolls came off, and it was a long time before I discovered that my own head would not fall off if I bent my neck. I used to walk around holding it very stiff because I thought a strong wind or a heavy push would snap my neck. Nel was the one who told me the truth. But she was wrong. I did not hold my head stiff enough when I met him and so I lost it just like the dolls.

"It's just as well he left. Soon I would have torn the flesh from his face just to see if I was right about the gold and nobody would have understood that kind of curiosity. They would have believed that I wanted to hurt him just like the little boy who fell down the steps and broke his leg and the people think I pushed him just because I looked at it."

Holding the driver's license she crawled into bed and fell into a sleep full of dreams of cobalt blue.

When she awoke, there was a melody in her head she could not identify or recall ever hearing before. "Perhaps I made it up," she thought. Then it came to her — the name of the song and all its lyrics just as she had heard it many times before. She sat on the edge of the bed thinking, "There aren't any more new songs and I have sung all the ones there are. I have sung them all.

I have sung all the songs there are." She lay down again on the bed and sang a little wandering tune made up of the words *I have sung all the songs all the songs I have sung all the songs there are* until, touched by her own lullaby, she grew drowsy, and in the hollow of near-sleep she tasted the acridness of gold, left the chill of alabaster and smelled the dark, sweet stench of loam.

1940

"I heard you was sick. Anything I can do for you?"

She had practiced not just the words but the tone, the pitch of her voice. It should be calm, matter-of-fact, but strong in sympathy — for the illness though, not for the patient.

The sound of her voice as she heard it in her head betrayed no curiosity, no pride, just the inflection of any good woman come to see about a sick person who, incidentally, had such visits from nobody else.

For the first time in three years she would be looking at the stemmed rose that hung over the eye of her enemy. Moreover, she would be doing it with the taste of Jude's exit in her mouth, with the resentment and shame that even yet pressed for release in her stomach. She would be facing the black rose that Jude had kissed and looking at the nostrils of the woman who had twisted her love for her own children into something so thick and monstrous she was afraid to show it lest it break loose and smother them with its heavy paw. A cumbersome bear-love that, given any rein, would suck their breath away in its crying need for honey.

Because Jude's leaving was so complete, the full responsibility of the household was Nel's. There were no more fifty dollars in brown envelopes to count on, so she took to cleaning rather than fret away the tiny seaman's pension her parents lived on. And just this past year she got a better job working as a chambermaid in the same hotel Jude had worked in. The tips were only fair, but the hours were good — she was home when the children got out of school.

At thirty her hot brown eyes had turned to agate, and her skin had taken on the sheen of maple struck down, split and sanded at the height of its green. Virtue, bleak and drawn, was her only mooring. It brought her to Number 7 Carpenter's Road and the door with the blue glass; it helped her to resist scratching the screen as in days gone by; it hid from her the true motives for her charity, and, finally, it gave her voice the timbre she wanted it to have:

free of delight or a lip-smacking "I told you so" with which the news of Sula's illness had been received up in the Bottom — free of the least hint of retribution.

Now she stood in Eva's old bedroom, looking down at that dark rose, aware of the knife-thin arms sliding back and forth over the quilt and the boarded-up window Eva had jumped out of.

Sula looked up and without a second's pause followed Nel's example of leaving out the greeting when she spoke.

"As a matter of fact, there is. I got a prescription. Nathan usually goes for me but he . . . school don't let out till three. Could you run it over to the drugstore?"

"Where is it?" Nel was glad to have a concrete errand. Conversation would be difficult. (Trust Sula to pick up a relationship exactly where it lay.)

"Look in my bag. No. Over there."

Nel walked to the dresser and opened the purse with the beaded clasp. She saw only a watch and the folded prescription down inside. No wallet, no change purse. She turned to Sula: "Where's your . . ."

But Sula was looking at the boarded-up window. Something in her eye right there in the corner stopped Nel from completing her question. That and the slight flare of the nostrils — a shadow of a snarl. Nel took the piece of paper and picked up her own purse, saying, "OK. I'll be right back."

As soon as the door was shut, Sula breathed through her mouth. While Nel was in the room the pain had increased. Now that this new pain killer, the one she had been holding in reserve, was on the way her misery was manageable. She let a piece of her mind lay on Nel. It was funny, sending Nel off to that drugstore right away like that, after she had not seen her to speak to for years. The drugstore was where Edna Finch's Mellow House used to be years back when they were girls. Where they used to go, the two of them, hand in hand, for the 18-cent ice-cream sundaes, past the Time and a Half Pool Hall, where the sprawling men said "pig meat," and they sat in that cool room with the marble-top tables and ate the first ice-cream sundaes of their lives. Now Nel was going back there alone and Sula was waiting for the medicine the doctor said not to take until the pain got really bad. And she supposed "really bad" was now. Although you could never tell. She wondered for an instant what Nellie wanted; why she had come. Did she want to gloat? Make up? Following this line of thought required more concentration than she could muster. Pain was greedy; it demanded all of her attention. But it was good that this new medicine, the reserve, would be brought to her by her old friend. Nel, she remembered, always thrived on a crisis. The closed place in the water; Hannah's funeral. Nel was the best. When Sula imitated her, or tried to, those long years ago, it always ended up in some action noteworthy not for its coolness but mostly for its being bizarre. The one time she tried to protect Nel, she had cut off her own finger tip and earned not Nel's gratitude but her disgust. From then on she had let her emotions dictate her behavior.

She could hear Nel's footsteps long before she opened the door and put the medicine on the table near the bed.

As Sula poured the liquid into a sticky spoon, Nel began the sickroom conversation.

"You look fine, Sula."

"You lying, Nellie. I look bad." She gulped the medicine.

"No. I haven't seen you for a long time, but you look . . ."

"You don't have to do that, Nellie. It's going to be all right."

"What ails you? Have they said?"

Sula licked the corners of her lips. "You want to talk about that?"

Nel smiled, slightly, at the bluntness she had forgotten. "No. No, I don't, but you sure you should be staying up here alone?"

"Nathan comes by. The deweys sometimes, and Tar Baby . . ."

"That ain't help, Sula. You need to be with somebody grown. Somebody who can . . ."

"I'd rather be here, Nellie."

"You know you don't have to be proud with me."

"Proud?" Sula's laughter broke through the phlegm. "What you talking about? I like my own dirt, Nellie. I'm not proud. You sure have forgotten me."

"Maybe. Maybe not. But you a woman and you alone."

"And you? Ain't you alone?"

"I'm not sick. I work."

"Yes. Of course you do. Work's good for you, Nellie. It don't do nothing for me."

"You never *had* to."

"I never would."

"There's something to say for it, Sula. 'Specially if you don't want people to have to do for you."

195

"Neither one, Nellie. Neither one."

"You can't have it all, Sula." Nel was getting exasperated with her arrogance, with her lying at death's door still smart-talking.

"Why? I can do it all, why can't I have it all?"

"You *can't* do it all. You a woman and a colored woman at that. You can't act like a man. You can't be walking around all independent-like, doing whatever you like, taking what you want, leaving what you don't."

"You repeating yourself."

"How repeating myself?"

"You say I'm a woman and colored. Ain't that the same as being a man?"

"I don't think so and you wouldn't either if you had children."

"Then I really would act like what you call a man. Every man I ever knew left his children."

"Some were taken."

"Wrong, Nellie. The word is 'left.' "

"You still going to know everything, ain't you?"

"I don't know everything, I just do everything."

"Well, you don't do what I do."

"You think I don't know what your life is like just because I ain't living it? I know

196

what every colored woman in this country is doing."

"What's that?"

"Dying. Just like me. But the difference is they dying like a stump. Me, I'm going down like one of those redwoods. I sure did live in this world."

"Really? What have you got to show for it?"

"Show? To who? Girl, I got my mind. And what goes on in it. Which is to say, I got me."

"Lonely, ain't it?"

"Yes. But my lonely is *mine*. Now your lonely is somebody else's. Made by somebody else and handed to you. Ain't that something? A secondhand lonely."

Nel sat back on the little wooden chair. Anger skipped but she realized that Sula was probably just showing off. No telling what shape she was really in, but there was no point in saying anything other than what was the truth. "I always understood how you could take a man. Now I understand why you can't keep none."

"Is that what I'm supposed to do? Spend my life keeping a man?"

"They worth keeping, Sula."

"They ain't worth more than me. And besides, I never loved no man because he was worth it. Worth didn't have nothing to do with it."

"What did?"

"My mind did. That's all."

"Well I guess that's it. You own the world and the rest of us is renting. You ride the pony and we shovel the shit. I didn't come up here for this kind of talk, Sula . . ."

"No?"

"No. I come to see about you. But now that you opened it up, I may as well close it." Nel's fingers closed around the brass rail of the bed. Now she would ask her. "How come you did it, Sula?"

There was a silence but Nel felt no obligation to fill it.

Sula stirred a little under the covers. She looked bored as she sucked her teeth. "Well, there was this space in front of me, behind me, in my head. Some space. And Jude filled it up. That's all. He just filled up the space."

"You mean you didn't even love him?" The feel of the brass was in Nel's mouth. "It wasn't even loving him?"

Sula looked toward the boarded-up window again. Her eyes fluttered as if she were about to fall off into sleep.

"But . . ." Nel held her stomach in. "But what about me? What about me? Why didn't you think about me? Didn't I count? I never hurt you. What did you take him for if you didn't love him and why didn't you think about me?" And then, "I was good to you, Sula, why don't that matter?"

Sula turned her head away from the boarded window. Her voice was quiet and the stemmed rose over her eye was very dark. "It matters, Nel, but only to you. Not to anybody else. Being good to somebody is just like being mean to somebody. Risky. You don't get nothing for it."

Nel took her hands from the brass railing. She was annoyed with herself. Finally when she had gotten the nerve to ask the question, the right question, it made no difference. Sula couldn't give her a sensible answer because she didn't know. Would be, in fact, the last to know. Talking to her about right and wrong was like talking to the deweys. She picked at the fringe on Sula's bedspread and said softly, "We were friends."

"Oh, yes. Good friends," Sula said.

"And you didn't love me enough to leave him alone. To let him love me. You had to take him away."

"What you mean take him away? I didn't kill him, I just fucked him. If we were such good friends, how come you couldn't get over it?"

"You laying there in that bed without a dime or a friend to your name having done all the dirt you did in this town and you still expect folks to love you?"

Sula raised herself up on her elbows. Her face glistened with the dew of fever. She opened her mouth as though to say something, then fell back on the pillows and sighed. "Oh, they'll love me all right. It will take time, but they'll love me." The sound of her voice was as soft and distant as the look in her eyes. "After all the old women have lain with the teen-agers; when all the young girls have slept with their old drunken uncles; after all the black men fuck all the white ones; when all the white women kiss all the black ones; when the guards have raped all the jailbirds and after all the whores make love to their grannies; after all the faggots get their mothers' trim; when Lindbergh sleeps with Bessie Smith and Norma Shearer makes it with Stepin Fetchit; after all the dogs have fucked all the cats and every weathervane on every barn flies off the roof to mount the hogs . . . then there'll be a little love left over for me. And I know just what it will feel like."

She closed her eyes then and thought of the wind pressing her dress between her legs as she ran up the bank of the river to four leaf-locked trees and the digging of holes in the earth.

Embarrassed, irritable and a little bit ashamed, Nel rose to go. "Goodbye, Sula. I don't reckon I'll be back."

She opened the door and heard Sula's low whisper. "Hey, girl." Nel paused and turned her head but not enough to see her.

"How you know?" Sula asked.

"Know what?" Nel still wouldn't look at her.

"About who was good. How you know it was you?"

"What you mean?"

"I mean maybe it wasn't you. Maybe it was me."

Nel took two steps out the door and closed it behind her. She walked down the hall and down the four flights of steps. The house billowed around her light then dark, full of presences without sounds. The deweys, Tar Baby, the newly married couples, Mr. Buckland Reed, Patsy, Valentine, and the beautiful Hannah Peace. Where were they? Eva out at the old folks' home, the deweys living anywhere, Tar Baby steeped in wine, and Sula upstairs in Eva's bed with a boarded-up window and an empty pocketbook on the dresser.

★ ★ ★

When Nel closed the door, Sula reached for more medicine. Then she turned the pillow over to its cool side and thought about her old friend. "So she will walk on down that road, her back so straight in that old green coat, the strap of her handbag pushed back all the way to the elbow, thinking how much I have cost her and never remember the days when we were two throats and one eye and we had no price."

Pictures drifted through her head as lightly as dandelion spores: the blue eagle that swallowed the E of the Sherman's Mellowe wine that Tar Baby drank; the pink underlid of Hannah's eye as she probed for a fleck of coal dust or a lash. She thought of looking out of the windows of all those trains and buses, looking at the feet and backs of all those people. Nothing was ever different. They were all the same. All of the words and all of the smiles, every tear and every gag just something to do.

"That's the same sun I looked at when I was twelve, the same pear trees. If I live a hundred years my urine will flow the same way, my armpits and breath will smell the same. My hair will grow from the same holes. I didn't mean anything. I never meant anything. I stood there watching her burn and was thrilled. I wanted her to keep on jerking like that, to keep on dancing."

Then she had the dream again. The Clabber Girl Baking Powder lady was smiling and beckoning to her, one hand under her apron. When Sula came near she disintegrated into white dust, which Sula was hurriedly trying to stuff into the pockets of her blue-flannel housecoat. The disintegration was awful to see, but worse was the feel of the powder — its starchy slipperiness as she tried to collect it by handfuls. The more she scooped, the more it billowed. At last it covered her, filled her eyes, her nose, her throat, and she woke gagging and overwhelmed with the smell of smoke.

Pain took hold. First a fluttering as of doves in her stomach, then a kind of burning, followed by a spread of thin wires to other parts of her body. Once the wires of liquid pain were in place, they jelled and began to throb. She tried concentrating on the throbs, identifying them as waves, hammer strokes, razor edges or small explosions. Soon even the variety of the pain bored her and there was nothing to do, for it was joined by fatigue so great she could not make a fist or fight the taste of oil at the back of her tongue.

Several times she tried to cry out, but

the fatigue barely let her open her lips, let alone take the deep breath necessary to scream. So she lay there wondering how soon she would gather enough strength to lift her arm and push the rough quilt away from her chin and whether she should turn her cheek to the cooler side of the pillow now or wait till her face was thoroughly soaked and the move would be more refreshing. But she was reluctant to move her face for another reason. If she turned her head, she would not be able to see the boarded-up window Eva jumped out of. And looking at those four wooden planks with the steel rod slanting across them was the only peace she had. The sealed window soothed her with its sturdy termination, its unassailable finality. It was as though for the first time she was completely alone — where she had always wanted to be — free of the possibility of distraction. It would be here, only here, held by this blind window high above the elm tree, that she might draw her legs up to her chest, close her eyes, put her thumb in her mouth and float over and down the tunnels, just missing the dark walls, down, down until she met a rain scent and would know the water was near, and she would curl into its heavy softness and it would envelop her, carry her, and wash her tired flesh always. Always. Who said that? She tried hard to think. Who was it that had promised her a sleep of water always? The effort to recall was too great; it loosened a knot in her chest that turned her thoughts again to the pain.

While in this state of weary anticipation, she noticed that she was not breathing, that her heart had stopped completely. A crease of fear touched her breast, for any second there was sure to be a violent explosion in her brain, a gasping for breath. Then she realized, or rather she sensed, that there was not going to be any pain. She was not breathing because she didn't have to. Her body did not need oxygen. She was dead.

Sula felt her face smiling, "Well, I'll be damned," she thought, "it didn't even hurt. Wait'll I tell Nel."

1941

The death of Sula Peace was the best news folks up in the Bottom had had since the promise of work at the tunnel. Of the few who were not afraid to witness the burial of a witch and who had gone to the cemetery, some had come just to verify her being put away but stayed to sing "Shall We Gather at the River" for politeness' sake, quite unaware of the bleak promise of their song. Others came to see that nothing went awry, that the shallow-minded and small-hearted kept their meanness at bay, and that the entire event be characterized by that abiding gentleness of spirit to which they themselves had arrived by the simple determination not to let anything — anything at all: not failed crops, not rednecks, lost jobs, sick children, rotten potatoes, broken pipes, bug-ridden flour, third-class coal, educated social workers, thieving insurance men, garlic-ridden hunkies, corrupt Catholics, racist

Protestants, cowardly Jews, slaveholding Moslems, jackleg nigger preachers, squeamish Chinamen, cholera, dropsy or the Black Plague, let alone a strange woman — keep them from their God.

In any case, both the raw-spirited and the gentle who came — not to the white funeral parlor but to the colored part of the Beechnut Cemetery — felt that either *because* Sula was dead or just *after* she was dead a brighter day was dawning. There were signs. The rumor that the tunnel spanning the river would use Negro workers became an announcement. Planned, abandoned and replanned for years, this project had finally begun in 1937. For three years there were rumors that blacks would work it, and hope was high in spite of the fact that the River Road leading to the tunnel had encouraged similar hopes in 1927 but had ended up being built entirely by white labor — hillbillies and immigrants taking even the lowest jobs. But the tunnel itself was another matter. The craft work — no, they would not get that. But it was a major job, and the government seemed to favor opening up employment to black workers. It meant black men would not have to sweep Medallion to eat, or leave the town altogether for the steel mills in Akron and along Lake Erie.

The second sign was the construction begun on an old people's home. True, it was more renovation than construction, but the blacks were free, or so it was said, to occupy it. Some said that the very transfer of Eva from the ramshackle house that passed for a colored women's nursing home to the bright new one was a clear sign of the mystery of God's ways, His mighty thumb having been seen at Sula's throat.

So it was with a strong sense of hope that the people in the Bottom watched October close.

Then Medallion turned silver. It seemed sudden, but actually there had been days and days of no snow — just frost — when, late one afternoon, a rain fell and froze. Way down Carpenter's Road, where the concrete sidewalks started, children hurried to the sliding places before shopkeepers and old women sprinkled stove ashes, like ancient onyx, onto the new-minted silver. They hugged trees simply to hold for a moment all that life and largeness stilled in glass, and gazed at the sun pressed against the gray sky like a worn doubloon, wondering all the while if the world were coming to an end. Grass stood blade by blade, shocked into separateness by an ice that held for days.

Late-harvesting things were ruined, of course, and fowl died of both chill and rage. Cider turned to ice and split the jugs, forcing the men to drink their cane liquor too soon. It was better down in the valley, since, as always, the hills protected it, but up in the Bottom black folks suffered heavily in their thin houses and thinner clothes. The ice-cold wind bled what little heat they had through windowpanes and ill-fitting doors. For days on end they were virtually housebound, venturing out only to coal-bins or right next door for the trading of vital foodstuffs. Never to the stores. No deliveries were being made anyway, and when they were, the items were saved for better-paying white customers. Women could not make it down the icy slopes and therefore missed days of wages they sorely needed.

The consequence of all that ice was a wretched Thanksgiving of tiny tough birds, heavy pork cakes, and pithy sweet potatoes. By the time the ice began to melt and the first barge was seen shuddering through the ice skim on the river, everybody under fifteen had croup, or scarlet fever, and those over had chilblains, rheumatism, pleurisy, earaches and a world of other ailments.

Still it was not those illnesses or even the ice that marked the beginning of the trouble, that self-fulfilled prophecy that Shadrack carried on his tongue. As soon as the silvering began, long before the cider cracked the jugs, there was something wrong. A falling away, a dislocation was taking place. Hard on the heels of the general relief that Sula's death brought a restless irritability took hold. Teapot, for example, went into the kitchen and asked his mother for some sugar-butter-bread. She got up to fix it and found that she had no butter, only oleomargarine. Too tired to mix the saffron-colored powder into the hard cake of oleo, she simply smeared the white stuff on the bread and sprinkled the sugar over it. Teapot tasted the difference and refused to eat it. This keenest of insults that a mother can feel, the rejection by a child of her food, bent her into fury and she beat him as she had not done since Sula knocked him down the steps. She was not alone. Other mothers who had defended their children from Sula's malevolence (or who had defended their positions as mothers from Sula's scorn for the role) now had nothing to rub up against. The tension was gone and so was the reason for the effort they had made. Without her mockery, affection for others sank into flaccid disrepair. Daughters who had complained bitterly about the responsibilities of taking care of their aged mothers-in-law had altered when Sula locked Eva away, and they began cleaning those old women's spittoons without a murmur. Now that Sula was dead and done with, they returned to a steeping resentment of the burdens of old people. Wives uncoddled their husbands; there seemed no further need to reinforce their vanity. And even those Negroes who had moved down from Canada to Medallion, who remarked every chance they got that they had never been slaves, felt a loosening of the reactionary compassion for Southern-born blacks Sula had inspired in them. They returned to their original claims of superiority.

The normal meanness that the winter brought was compounded by the small-spiritedness that hunger and scarlet fever produced. Even a definite and witnessed interview of four colored men (and the promise of more in the spring) at the tunnel site could not break the cold vise of that lean and bitter year's end.

Christmas came one morning and haggled everybody's nerves like a dull ax — too shabby to cut clean but too heavy to ignore. The children lay wall-eyed on creaking beds or pallets near the stove, sucking peppermint and oranges in between coughs while their mothers stomped the floors in rage at the cakes that did not rise because the stove fire had been so stingy; at the curled bodies of men who chose to sleep the day away rather than face the silence made by the absence of Lionel trains, drums, crybaby dolls and rocking horses. Teen-agers sneaked into the Elmira Theater in the afternoon and let Tex Ritter free them from the recollection of their fathers' shoes, yawning in impotence under the bed. Some of them had a bottle of wine, which they drank at the feet of the glittering Mr. Ritter, making such a ruckus the manager had to put them out. The white people who came with Christmas bags of rock candy and old clothes were hard put to get a *Yes'm, thank you,* out of those sullen mouths.

Just as the ice lingered in October, so did the phlegm of December — which explained the enormous relief brought on by the first three days of 1941. It was as though the season had exhausted itself, for on January first the temperature shot up to sixty-one degrees and slushed the whiteness overnight. On January second drab patches of grass could be seen in the fields. On January third the sun came out — and so did Shadrack with his rope, his bell and his childish dirge.

He had spent the night before watching a tiny moon. The people, the voices that kept him company, were with him less and less. Now there were long periods when he heard nothing except the wind in the trees and the plop of buckeyes on the earth. In the winter, when the fish were too hard to get to, he did picking-up jobs for small businessmen (nobody would have him in or even near their homes), and thereby continued to have enough money for liquor. Yet the drunk times were becoming deeper but more seldom. It was as though he no longer needed to drink to forget whatever it was he could not remember. Now he could not remember that he had ever forgotten anything. Perhaps that was why for the first time after that cold day in France he was beginning to miss the presence of other people. Shadrack had improved enough to feel lonely. If he was lonely before, he didn't know it because the noise he kept up, the roaring, the busyness, protected him from knowing it. Now the compulsion to activity, to filling up the time when he was not happily fishing on the riverbank, had dwindled. He sometimes fell asleep before he got drunk; sometimes spent whole days looking at the river and the sky; and more and more he relinquished the military habits of cleanliness in his shack. Once a bird flew into his door — one of the robins during the time there was a plague of them. It stayed, looking for an exit, for the better part of an hour. When the bird found the window and flew away, Shadrack was grieved and actually waited and watched for its return. During those days of waiting, he did not make his bed, or sweep, or shake out the little rag-braid rug, and almost forgot to slash with his fish knife the passing day on his calendar. When he did return to housekeeping, it was not with the precision he had always insisted upon. The messier his house got, the lonelier he felt, and it was harder and harder to conjure up sergeants, and orderlies, and invading armies; harder and harder to hear the gunfire and keep the platoon marching in time. More frequently now he looked at and fondled the one piece of evidence that he once had a visitor in his house: a child's purple-and-white belt. The one the little girl left behind when she came to see him. Shadrack remembered the scene clearly. He had stepped into the door and there was a tear-stained face turning, turning toward him; eyes hurt and wondering; mouth parted in an effort to ask a question. She had wanted something — from him. Not fish, not work, but something only he could give. She had a tadpole over her eye (that was how he knew she was a friend — she had the mark of the fish he loved), and one of her braids had come undone. But when he looked at her face he had seen also the skull beneath, and thinking she saw it too — knew it was there and was afraid — he tried to think of something to say to comfort her, something to stop the hurt from spilling out of her eyes. So he had said "always," so she would not have to be afraid of the change — the falling away of skin, the drip and slide of blood, and the exposure of bone underneath. He had said "always" to convince her, assure her, of permanency.

It worked, for when he said it her face lit up and the hurt did leave. She ran then, carrying his knowledge, but her belt fell off and he kept it as a memento. It hung on a nail near his bed — unfrayed, unsullied after all those years, with only the permanent bend in the fabric made by its long life on a nail. It was pleasant living with that sign of a visitor, his only one. And after a while he was able to connect the belt with the face, the tadpole-over-the-eye-face that he sometimes saw up in the Bottom. His visitor, his company, his guest, his social life, his woman, his daughter, his friend — they all hung there on a nail near his bed.

Now he stared at the tiny moon floating high over the ice-choked river. His loneliness had dropped down somewhere around his ankles. Some other feeling possessed him. A feeling that touched his eyes and made him blink. He had seen her again months? weeks? ago. Raking leaves for Mr. Hodges, he had gone into the cellar for two bushel baskets to put them in. In the hallway he passed an open door leading to a small room. She lay on a table there. It was surely the same one. The same little-girl face, same tadpole over the eye. So he had been wrong. Terribly wrong. No "always" at all. Another dying away of someone whose face he knew.

It was then he began to suspect that all

those years of rope hauling and bell ringing were never going to do any good. He might as well sit forever on his riverbank and stare out of the window at the moon.

By his day-slashed calendar he knew that tomorrow was the day. And for the first time he did not want to go. He wanted to stay with the purple-and-white belt. Not go. Not go.

Still, when the day broke in an incredible splash of sun, he gathered his things. In the early part of the afternoon, drenched in sunlight and certain that this would be the last time he would invite them to end their lives neatly and sweetly, he walked over the rickety bridge and on into the Bottom. But it was not heartfelt this time, not loving this time, for he no longer cared whether he helped them or not. His rope was improperly tied; his bell had a tinny unimpassioned sound. His visitor was dead and would come no more.

Years later people would quarrel about who had been the first to go. Most folks said it was the deweys, but one or two knew better, knew that Dessie and Ivy had been first. Said that Dessie had opened her door first and stood there shielding her eyes from the sun while watching Shadrack coming down the road. She laughed.

Maybe the sun; maybe the clots of green showing in the hills promising so much; maybe the contrast between Shadrack's doomy, gloomy bell glinting in all that sweet sunshine. Maybe just a brief moment, for once, of not feeling fear, of looking at death in the sunshine and being unafraid. She laughed.

Upstairs, Ivy heard her and looked to see what caused the thick music that rocked her neighbor's breasts. Then Ivy laughed too. Like the scarlet fever that had touched everybody and worn them down to gristle, their laughter infected Carpenter's Road. Soon children were jumping about giggling and men came to the porches to chuckle. By the time Shadrack reached the first house, he was facing a line of delighted faces.

Never before had they laughed. Always they had shut their doors, pulled down the shades and called their children out of the road. It frightened him, this glee, but he stuck to his habit — singing his song, ringing his bell and holding fast to his rope. The deweys with their magnificent teeth ran out from Number 7 and danced a little jig around the befuddled Shadrack, then cut into a wild aping of his walk, his song and his bell-ringing. By now women were holding their stomachs, and the men were slapping their knees. It was Mrs. Jackson, who ate ice, who tripped down off her porch and marched — actually marched — along behind him. The scene was so comic the people walked into the road to make sure they saw it all. In that way the parade started.

Everybody, Dessie, Tar Baby, Patsy, Mr. Buckland Reed, Teapot's Mamma, Valentine, the deweys, Mrs. Jackson, Irene, the proprietor of the Palace of Cosmetology, Reba, the Herrod brothers and flocks of teen-agers got into the mood and, laughing, dancing, calling to one another, formed a pied piper's band behind Shadrack. As the initial group of about twenty people passed more houses, they called to the people standing in doors and leaning out of windows to join them; to help them open further this slit in the veil, this respite from anxiety, from dignity, from gravity, from the weight of that very adult pain that had undergirded them all those years before. Called to them to come out and play in the sunshine — as though the sunshine would last, as though there really was hope. The same hope that kept them

219

picking beans for other farmers; kept them from finally leaving as they talked of doing; kept them knee-deep in other people's dirt; kept them excited about other people's wars; kept them solicitous of white people's children; kept them convinced that some magic "government" was going to lift them up, out and away from that dirt, those beans, those wars.

Some, of course, like Helene Wright, would not go. She watched the ruckus with characteristic scorn. Others, who understood the Spirit's touch which made them dance, who understood whole families bending their backs in a field while singing as from one throat, who understood the ecstasy of river baptisms under suns just like this one, did not understand this curious disorder, this headless display and so refused also to go.

Nevertheless, the sun splashed on a larger and larger crowd that strutted, skipped, marched, and shuffled down the road. When they got down to where the sidewalk started, some of them stopped and decided to turn back, too embarrassed to enter the white part of town whooping like banshees. But except for three or four, the fainthearted were put to shame by the more aggressive and abandoned, and the parade danced down Main Street past Woolworth's and the old poultry house, turned right and moved on down the New River Road.

At the mouth of the tunnel excavation, in a fever pitch of excitement and joy, they saw the timber, the bricks, the steel ribs and the tacky wire gate that glittered under ice struck to diamond in the sun. It dazzled them, at first, and they were suddenly quiet. Their hooded eyes swept over the place where their hope had lain since 1927. There was the promise: leaf-dead. The teeth unrepaired, the coal credit cut off, the chest pains unattended, the school shoes unbought, the rush-stuffed mattresses, the broken toilets, the leaning porches, the slurred remarks and the staggering childish malevolence of their employers. All there in blazing sunlit ice rapidly becoming water.

Like antelopes they leaped over the little gate — a wire barricade that was never intended to bar anything but dogs, rabbits and stray children — and led by the tough, the enraged and the young they picked up the lengths of timber and thin steel ribs and smashed the bricks they would never fire in yawning kilns, split the sacks of limestone they had not mixed or even been allowed to haul; tore the wire mesh, tipped over wheelbarrows and rolled forepoles down the bank, where they sailed far out on the icebound river.

Old and young, women and children, lame and hearty, they killed, as best they could, the tunnel they were forbidden to build.

They didn't mean to go in, to actually go down into the lip of the tunnel, but in their need to kill it all, all of it, to wipe from the face of the earth the work of the thin-armed Virginia boys, the bull-necked Greeks and the knife-faced men who waved the leaf-dead promise, they went too deep, too far . . .

A lot of them died there. The earth, now warm, shifted; the first forepole slipped; loose rock fell from the face of the tunnel and caused a shield to give way. They found themselves in a chamber of water, deprived of the sun that had brought them there. With the first crack and whoosh of water, the clamber to get out was so fierce that others who were trying to help were pulled to their deaths. Pressed up against steel ribs and timber blocks young boys strangled when the oxygen left them to join the water. Outside, others watched in terror as ice split and earth shook beneath their feet. Mrs. Jackson, weighing less than 100 pounds, slid down the bank and met with an open mouth the ice she had craved all her life. Tar Baby, Dessie, Ivy, Valentine, the Herrod boys, some of Ajax's younger brothers and the deweys (at least it was supposed; their bodies were never found) — all died there. Mr. Buckland Reed escaped, so did Patsy and her two boys, as well as some fifteen or twenty who had not gotten close enough to fall, or whose timidity would not let them enter an unfinished tunnel.

And all the while Shadrack stood there. Having forgotten his song and his rope, he just stood there high up on the bank ringing, ringing his bell.

1965

Things were so much better in 1965. Or so it seemed. You could go downtown and see colored people working in the dime store behind the counters, even handling money with cash-register keys around their necks. And a colored man taught mathematics at the junior high school. The young people had a look about them that everybody said was new but which reminded Nel of the deweys, whom nobody had ever found. Maybe, she thought, they had gone off and seeded the land and growed up in these young people in the dime store with the cash-register keys around their necks.

They were so different, these young people. So different from the way she remembered them forty years ago.

Jesus, there were some beautiful boys in 1921! Look like the whole world was bursting at the seams with them. Thirteen, fourteen, fifteen years old. Jesus, they were fine. L.P., Paul Freeman and his brother Jake, Mrs. Scott's twins — and Ajax had a whole flock of younger brothers. They hung out of attic windows, rode on car fenders, delivered the coal, moved into Medallion and moved out, visited cousins, plowed, hoisted, lounged on the church steps, careened on the school playground. The sun heated them and the moon slid down their backs. God, the world was *full* of beautiful boys in 1921.

Nothing like these kids. Everything had changed. Even the whores were better then: tough, fat, laughing women with burns on their cheeks and wit married to their meanness: or widows couched in small houses in the woods with eight children to feed and no man. These modern-day whores were pale and dull before those women. These little clothes-crazy things were always embarrassed. Nasty but shamed. They didn't know what shameless was. They should have known those silvery widows in the woods who would get up from the dinner table and walk into the trees with a customer with as much embarrassment as a calving mare.

Lord, how time flies. She hardly recognized anybody in the town any more. Now there was another old people's home. Look like this town just kept on building homes for old people. Every time they built a road they built a old folks' home. You'd think folks was living longer, but the fact of it was, they was just being put out faster.

Nel hadn't seen the insides of this most recent one yet, but it was her turn in Circle Number 5 to visit some of the old women there. The pastor visited them regularly, but the circle thought private visits were nice too. There were just nine colored women out there, the same nine that had been in the other one. But a lot of white ones. White people didn't fret about putting their old ones away. It took a lot for black people to let them go, and even if somebody was old and alone, others did the dropping by, the floor washing, the cooking. Only when they got crazy and un-manageable were they let go. Unless it was somebody like Sula, who put Eva away out of meanness. It was true that Eva was foolish in the head, but not so bad as to need locking up.

Nel was more than a little curious to see her. She had been really active in church only a year or less, and that was because the children were grown now and took up less time and less space in her mind. For over twenty-five years since Jude walked out she had pinned herself into a tiny life. She spent a little time trying to marry again, but nobody wanted to take her on with three children, and she simply couldn't manage the business of keeping boyfriends. During the war she had had a rather long relationship with a sergeant stationed at the camp twenty miles down river from Medallion, but then he got called away and everything was reduced to a few letters — then nothing. Then there was a bartender at the hotel. But now she was fifty-five and hard put to remember what all that had been about.

It didn't take long, after Jude left, for her to see what the future would be. She had looked at her children and knew in her heart that that would be all. That they were all she would ever know of love. But it was a love that, like a pan of syrup kept too long on the stove, had cooked out, leaving only its odor and a hard, sweet sludge, impossible to scrape off. For the mouths of her children quickly forgot the taste of her nipples, and years ago they had begun to look past her face into the nearest stretch of sky.

In the meantime the Bottom had collapsed. Everybody who had made money during the war moved as close as they could to the valley, and the white people were buying down river, cross river, stretching Medallion like two strings on the banks. Nobody colored lived much up in the Bottom any more. White people were building towers for television stations up there and there was a rumor about a golf course or something. Anyway, hill land was more valuable now, and those black people who had moved down right after the war and in the fifties couldn't afford to come back even if they wanted to. Except for the few blacks still huddled by the river bend, and some undemolished houses on Carpenter's Road, only rich white folks were building homes in the hills. Just like that, they had changed their minds and instead of keeping the valley floor to themselves, now they wanted a hilltop house with a river view and a ring of elms. The black people, for all their new look, seemed awfully anxious to get to the valley, or leave town, and abandon the hills to whoever was interested. It was sad, because the Bottom had been a real place. These young ones kept talking about the community, but they left the hills to the poor, the old, the stubborn — and the rich white folks. Maybe it hadn't been a community, but it had been a place. Now there weren't any places left, just separate houses with separate televisions and separate telephones and less and less dropping by.

These were the same thoughts she always had when she walked down into the town. One of the last true pedestrians, Nel walked the shoulder road while cars slipped by. Laughed at by her children, she still walked wherever she wanted to go, allowing herself to accept rides only when the weather required it.

Now she went straight through the town and turned left at its farthest end, along a tree-lined walk that turned into a country road farther on and passed the cemetery, Beechnut Park.

When she got to Sunnydale, the home for the aged, it was already four o'clock and turning chill. She would be glad to sit down with those old birds and rest her feet.

A red-haired lady at the desk gave her a pass card and pointed to a door that opened onto a corridor of smaller doors. It looked like what she imagined a college dormitory to be. The lobby was luxurious — modern — but the rooms she peeped into were sterile green cages. There was too much light everywhere; it needed some shadows. The third door, down the hall, had a little name tag over it that read EVA PEACE. Nel twisted the knob and rapped a little on the door at the same time, then listened a moment before she opened it.

At first she couldn't believe it. She seemed so small, sitting at that table in a black-vinyl chair. All the heaviness had gone and the height. Her once beautiful leg had no stocking and the foot was in a slipper. Nel wanted to cry — not for Eva's milk-dull eyes or her floppy lips, but for the once proud foot accustomed for over a half century to a fine well-laced shoe, now stuffed gracelessly into a pink terrycloth slipper.

"Good evening, Miss Peace. I'm Nel Greene come to pay a call on you. You remember me, don't you?"

Eva was ironing and dreaming of stairwells. She had neither iron nor clothes but did not stop her fastidious lining up of pleats or pressing out of wrinkles even when she acknowledged Nel's greeting.

"Howdy. Sit down."

"Thank you." Nel sat on the edge of the little bed. "You've got a pretty room, a real pretty room, Miss Peace."

"You eat something funny today?"

"Ma'am?"

"Some chop suey? Think back."

"No, ma'am."

"No? Well, you gone be sick later on."

"But I didn't have no chop suey."

"You think I come all the way over here for you to tell me that? I can't make visits too often. You should have some respect for old people."

"But Miss Peace, I'm visiting *you*. This is *your* room." Nel smiled.

"What you say your name was?"

"Nel Greene."

"Wiley Wright's girl?"

"Uh huh. You do remember. That makes me feel good, Miss Peace. You remember me and my father."

"Tell me how you killed that little boy."

"What? What little boy?"

"The one you threw in the water. I got oranges. How did you get him to go in the water?"

"I didn't throw no little boy in the river. That was Sula."

"You. Sula. What's the difference? You was there. You watched, didn't you? Me, I never would've watched."

"You're confused, Miss Peace. I'm Nel. Sula's dead."

"It's awful cold in the water. Fire is warm. How did you get him in?" Eva wet her forefinger and tested the iron's heat.

"Who told you all these lies? Miss Peace? Who told you? Why are you telling lies on me?"

"I got oranges. I don't drink they old orange juice. They puts something in it."

"Why are you trying to make out like I did it?"

Eva stopped ironing and looked at Nel. For the first time her eyes looked sane.

"You think I'm guilty?" Nel was whispering.

Eva whispered back, "Who would know that better than you?"

"I want to know who you been talking to." Nel forced herself to speak normally.

"Plum. Sweet Plum. He tells me things." Eva laughed a light, tinkly giggle — girlish.

"I'll be going now, Miss Peace." Nel stood.

"You ain't answered me yet."

"I don't know what you're talking about."

"Just alike. Both of you. Never was no difference between you. Want some oranges? It's better for you than chop suey. Sula? I got oranges."

Nel walked hurriedly down the hall, Eva calling after her, "Sula?" Nel couldn't see the other women today. That woman had upset her. She handed her pass back to the lady, avoiding her look of surprise.

Outside she fastened her coat against the rising wind. The top button was missing so she covered her throat with her hand. A bright space opened in her head and memory seeped into it.

Standing on the riverbank in a purple-and-white dress, Sula swinging Chicken Little around and around. His laughter before the hand-slip and the water closing quickly over the place. What had she felt then, watching Sula going around and around and then the little boy swinging out over the water? Sula had cried and cried when she came back from Shadrack's house. But Nel had remained calm.

"Shouldn't we tell?"

"Did he see?"

"I don't know. No."

"Let's go. We can't bring him back."

What did old Eva mean by *you watched?* How could she help seeing it? She was right there. But Eva didn't say *see,* she said *watched.* "I did not watch it. I just saw it." But it was there anyway, as it had always been, the old feeling and the old question. The good feeling she had had when Chicken's hands slipped. She hadn't wondered about that in years. "Why didn't I feel bad when it happened? How come it felt so good to see him fall?"

All these years she had been secretly proud of her calm, controlled behavior when Sula was uncontrollable, her compassion for Sula's frightened and shamed eyes. Now it seemed that what she had thought was maturity, serenity and compassion was only the tranquillity that follows a joyful stimulation. Just as the water closed peacefully over the turbulence of Chicken Little's body, so had contentment washed over her enjoyment.

She was walking too fast. Not watching where she placed her feet, she got into the weeds by the side of the road. Running almost, she approached Beechnut Park. Just over there was the colored part of the cemetery. She went in. Sula was buried there along with Plum, Hannah and now Pearl. With the same disregard for name changes by marriage that the black people of Medallion always showed, each flat slab had one word carved on it. Together they read like a chant: PEACE 1895–1921, PEACE 1890–1923, PEACE 1910–1940, PEACE 1892–1959.

They were not dead people. They were words. Not even words. Wishes, longings.

All these years she had been harboring good feelings about Eva; sharing, she believed, her loneliness and unloved state as no one else could or did. She, after all, was the only one who really understood why Eva refused to attend Sula's funeral. The others thought they knew; thought the grandmother's reasons were the same as their own — that to pay respect to someone who had caused them so much pain was beneath them. Nel, who did go, believed Eva's refusal was not due to pride or vengeance but to a plain unwillingness to see the swallowing of her own flesh into the dirt, a determination not to let the eyes see what the heart could not hold.

Now, however, after the way Eva had just treated her, accused her, she wondered if the townspeople hadn't been right the first time. Eva *was* mean. Sula had even said so. There was no good reason for her to speak so. Feebleminded or not. Old. Whatever. Eva knew what she was doing. Always had. She had stayed away from Sula's funeral and accused Nel of drowning Chicken Little for spite. The same spite that galloped all over the Bottom. That made every gesture an offense, every off-center smile a threat, so that even the bubbles of relief that broke in the chest of practically everybody when Sula died did not soften their spite and allow them to go to Mr.

Hodges' funeral parlor or send flowers from the church or bake a yellow cake.

She thought about Nathan opening the bedroom door the day she had visited her, and finding the body. He said he knew she was dead right away not because her eyes were open but because her mouth was. It looked to him like a giant yawn that she never got to finish. He had run across the street to Teapot's Mamma, who, when she heard the news, said, "Ho!" like the conductor on the train when it was about to take off except louder, and then did a little dance. None of the women left their quilt patches in disarray to run to the house. Nobody left the clothes halfway through the wringer to run to the house. Even the men just said "uhn," when they heard. The day passed and no one came. The night slipped into another day and the body was still lying in Eva's bed gazing at the ceiling trying to complete a yawn. It was very strange, this stubbornness about Sula. For even when China, the most rambunctious whore in the town, died (whose black son and white son said, when they heard she was dying, "She ain't dead yet?"), even then everybody stopped what they were doing and turned out in numbers to put the fallen sister away.

It was Nel who finally called the hospital, then the mortuary, then the police, who were the ones to come. So the white people took over. They came in a police van and carried the body down the steps past the four pear trees and into the van for all the world as with Hannah. When the police asked questions nobody gave them any information. It took them hours to find out the dead woman's first name. The call was for a Miss Peace at 7 Carpenter's Road. So they left with that: a body, a name and an address. The white people had to wash her, dress her, prepare her and finally lower her. It was all done elegantly, for it was discovered that she had a substantial death policy. Nel went to the funeral parlor, but was so shocked by the closed coffin she stayed only a few minutes.

The following day Nel walked to the burying and found herself the only black person there, steeling her mind to the roses and pulleys. It was only when she turned to leave that she saw the cluster of black folk at the lip of the cemetery. Not coming in, not dressed for mourning, but there waiting. Not until the white folks left — the gravediggers, Mr. and Mrs. Hodges, and their young son who assisted them —

did those black people from up in the Bottom enter with hooded hearts and filed eyes to sing "Shall We Gather at the River" over the curved earth that cut them off from the most magnificent hatred they had ever known. Their question clotted the October air, Shall We Gather at the River? The beautiful, the beautiful river? Perhaps Sula answered them even then, for it began to rain, and the women ran in tiny leaps through the grass for fear their straightened hair would beat them home.

Sadly, heavily, Nel left the colored part of the cemetery. Further along the road Shadrack passed her by. A little shaggier, a little older, still energetically mad, he looked at the woman hurrying along the road with the sunset in her face.

He stopped. Trying to remember where he had seen her before. The effort of recollection was too much for him and he moved on. He had to haul some trash out at Sunnydale and it would be good and dark before he got home. He hadn't sold fish in a long time now. The river had killed them all. No more silver-gray flashes, no more flat, wide, unhurried look. No more slowing down of gills. No more tremor on the line.

Shadrack and Nel moved in opposite directions, each thinking separate thoughts about the past. The distance between them increased as they both remembered gone things.

Suddenly Nel stopped. Her eye twitched and burned a little.

"Sula?" she whispered, gazing at the tops of trees. "Sula?"

Leaves stirred; mud shifted; there was the smell of overripe green things. A soft ball of fur broke and scattered like dandelion spores in the breeze.

"All that time, all that time, I thought I was missing Jude." And the loss pressed down on her chest and came up into her throat. "We was girls together," she said as though explaining something. "O Lord, Sula," she cried, "girl, girl, girlgirlgirl."

It was a fine cry — loud and long — but it had no bottom and it had no top, just circles and circles of sorrow.